Painting Mr. Darcy

A Pride and Prejudice Variation

GRACE HOLLISTER

Painting Mr. Darcy
Grace Hollister
Copyright © 2018
All Rights Reserved.

Cover design: Grace Hollister
Editor: Miss Editrix and Mystique Editing

For my darling husband and kids.

CHAPTER 1

Elizabeth Bennet was enjoying her morning walk in the garden of the Hunsford Parsonage when the hairs at the back of her neck rose. A feeling of unease settled upon her, similar to when she suspected that she was being observed without her knowledge.

Holding her breath, she turned to look behind her, squinting into the distance. The piercing sunlight of early morning made it difficult for her to make out the person coming towards her. She raised her hand to shield her eyes from the glare of the sun just as the figure emerged and became more visible.

Her heart stuttered when she noticed who it was.

Mr. Darcy. What would bring him here

so early in the morning?

As he strode towards her, she suddenly recalled a conversation with him the night before, when Mr. and Mrs. Collins had invited him and Colonel Fitzwilliam to supper.

Similar to their previous conversations, he had been rather distant and aloof. Since the Meryton Ball, Elizabeth's opinion of him had only worsened and she would admit to finding him as disagreeable as ever. Not only was she appalled at how he had treated Mr. Wickham, she was infuriated to discover that he also played a role in keeping her sister Jane and her beloved Mr. Bingley apart.

What Colonel Fitzwilliam had told her during their brief conversation after supper, had only confirmed Elizabeth's opinion of the kind of man Mr. Darcy really was.

Colonel Fitzwilliam had hinted that Mr. Darcy had been involved in orchestrating the separation of Jane and Mr. Bingley. Though he had not mentioned the two by name, Elizabeth was clever enough to unveil the shadowed truth.

The more distance Mr. Darcy closed between them, the more her heart sank with trepidation.

After breakfast with the Collinses, Elizabeth had been looking forward to a solitary stroll, to seek understanding with all that she had heard from Colonel Fitzwilliam. She had always found joy in her walks, and now the last person she wished to speak with was disturbing her peace.

"Miss Bennet," he said with a polite bow of his head, when he was close enough to be heard. A corner of his lips twitched as he folded his hands in front of him, pretending to be a gentleman even though she could see right through him. Gentlemen were kind and generous, and Mr. Darcy was neither.

"Good morning, Mr. Darcy. I had no idea you would call again so soon after yesterday's supper."

"Neither did I," he said. "I hope you're doing well this morning."

Elizabeth's lips curled with a smile that failed to reach her eyes. "I would be doing much better had I not been disturbed during my morning walk."

"Then I must apologize for disturbing you." Mr. Darcy shifted from one foot to the other, his gaze lowering for a brief moment. When he looked up again, his eyes rested on her face.

Elizabeth was horrified when a wave of unexpected warmth flooded her cheeks. As much as she wished to deny it, there was something about Mr. Darcy which unraveled her most disconcertingly. She hated that the man had such an effect on her, especially one she could not understand.

"Did you come to see Mr. and Mrs. Collins?" she asked to break the awkward silence.

"I am afraid not. It is you I came to see, Miss Bennet." He plucked a green leaf from the low hanging branch of a nearby tree and attempted to toss it into the pond. It landed at his feet instead. He straightened to his full height and cleared his throat. "I'd been meaning to talk to you after supper yesterday."

Elizabeth tipped her head to the side. "I do not understand what more we could have spoken about. As I recall, we had thoroughly discussed the beauty of Kent. I cannot imagine any other topics that would be of interest to the both of us."

Seated next to Mr. Darcy at the table yesterday, Elizabeth had refused to discuss anything of a personal nature and had, instead, leaned on mundane topics like the weather and their surroundings. All the while, she had prayed for supper to end before she lost her composure and told Mr. Darcy exactly what she thought of him.

Mr. Darcy averted his gaze. "Miss Bennet, I must be honest with you, my character demands it. I had ulterior motives for accepting Mr. and Mrs. Collins's invitation to supper. It was you I had hoped to see."

"Is that so? What is it you wished to talk to me about, Mr. Darcy? I assure you I can think of no reason." Elizabeth turned away from him to face the pond, her focus on the sparkle on the surface of the water. Looking into his eyes would unsettle her in a way she did not approve of.

A smile snuck onto her lips as she

listened to his feet shifting. It pleased her to think she was causing him as much discomfort as he was her. "Mr. Darcy, I would ask for you to be direct. What is it you wanted to say to me yesterday?" She turned her head slightly to peer at his face. "It surprises me that you would want to speak to someone belonging to a family you find so despicable."

He didn't speak for a while and she did not feel the need to fill the silence to ease his discomfort. Did he truly believe she would not learn that he was the person behind Jane's unhappiness?

"Miss Bennet, am I wrong in thinking there is something you would like to discuss with me as well?"

Elizabeth drew in a deep breath and turned to face him, her arms wrapped around herself as though she were cold. "Indeed, Mr. Darcy. There is plenty I would like to say to you."

"In that case, I am glad I visited again so we can continue our conversation." His face showed no sign of remorse.

"Perhaps we could discuss the topic of secrets and how they do not stay hidden for long. They have a way of coming out into the open, wouldn't you agree?" Elizabeth allowed a faint smile to touch her lips. "Do you happen to be keeping any secrets of your own, Mr. Darcy?"

"I do not know what you mean." He placed a finger on his lips, puzzled. "I do not consider myself to be a man of secrets."

"Is that so?" Elizabeth shook her head in confusion. "Is it not true that you were the person who discouraged Mr. Bingley from exploring his feelings for my sister? Is it also not true that you consider my family to be beneath you?"

"Miss Bennet, as much as I consider myself to be a man of no secrets, I also pride myself on being truthful." Mr. Darcy's face tightened. "The truth is, Mr. Bingley had asked for my advice regarding the matter, and as a good friend, I simply gave him my honest opinion."

Mounting rage sent a wave of heat up Elizabeth's neck. "Your honest opinion about disliking my family to such a degree that you found it would be unbearable for Mr. Bingley to consider being a part of it?"

Mr. Darcy sighed. "Please do not misunderstand me, Miss Bennet. I do not have any ill feelings toward your sister... or you. But your mother and—"

Elizabeth raised a hand to stop him from throwing another arrow at her heart. "Mr. Darcy, I think it is best we end this conversation before regretful things are said. Do you not agree? The truth is, I have as much to say about you as you have to say about my family."

He took one step back as though she had struck him. "I do apologize if I came across as unpleasant to you. I can assure you that your opinion of me is not one I feel is warranted. And one I find myself hoping you may soon change. But perhaps it is best we do not discuss your family. I would rather you give me the opportunity to tell you what I came here to say."

Elizabeth raised an eyebrow. "You mean to say you did not come to make further foolery of me and my family? I have to say that surprises me a great deal."

"It should not." He unfolded his hands and allowed them to hang by his side. "What I have to say has to do with my feelings for—"

Whatever he had meant to say was disturbed by the sound of someone calling Elizabeth's name. Startled, they both turned in the direction of the voice to see Mr. Collins walking briskly towards them. By the time he reached the pair, he was quite out of breath.

Elizabeth rested the palm of her hand on her chest and frowned. "Mr. Collins, is everything all right?"

Mr. Collins took a few breaths to calm himself down and used the back of his hand to wipe away the sheen of sweat on his brow. "Miss Elizabeth, I am afraid I have some unpleasant news."

"Unpleasant news? What kind?" Elizabeth's gaze fell onto the crumpled page in Mr. Collins's hand. It looked like a letter. "Is that the bearer of ill news?"

Mr. Collins gazed briefly at Mr. Darcy as though silently requesting a moment alone with Elizabeth.

Mr. Darcy understood his look immediately and nodded, and stepped away, but instead of journeying to the house, he roamed the garden not too far from where Elizabeth and Mr. Collins stood.

Mr. Collins turned to Elizabeth, his face as crumpled as the letter in his hand. He waved the letter in the space between them, though he did not offer it to Elizabeth. "This was sent to me by Mr. Bennet. He requests that you return to Longbourn at once. He thought it best to write to me instead of you as the news is devastating."

"I do not understand." Elizabeth glanced at Mr. Darcy in the distance and then back at Mr. Collins. "What is so urgent that I am requested to leave immediately? I have not been here for long. I would appreciate it if you shared with me the entire contents of my father's letter." She felt her chest tighten. As much as she wished to know, she was afraid it was the kind of news she would not be able to handle.

"Miss Elizabeth, I am sad to say your father has fallen ill," said Mr. Collins.

The news struck Elizabeth like a bolt of lightning. In response, her heart clenched and her shoulders caved in. "Did he say what kind of illness has befallen him?" In her despair, she found it hard to even utter the words. The mere thought of her dear father suffering from any kind of illness was unbearable.

"I am afraid not." Mr. Collins took Elizabeth's arm as though to comfort her, but he released it just as quickly. "The letter simply states that he is gravely ill, and he wishes for your return."

"Gravely ill?" Elizabeth's fingers fluttered to her throat, as she struggled to breathe. Through the blur in her eyes, she watched Mr. Collins as he continued speaking, but his words were distorted by the rush in her ears.

"Miss Elizabeth?" Mr. Collins's voice sounded as though it were coming from a distance away. "Are you all right?"

"I am afraid not, Mr. Collins." Elizabeth drew in a breath. "Of course I shall return to Longbourn immediately to be at my father's side."

Mr. Collins nodded and tightened his fingers around the letter. "In that case, I shall make all the necessary arrangements for your departure with haste."

Elizabeth nodded. "Thank you. I shall prepare for my journey."

Mr. Collins rushed off again, and Elizabeth could not help the unkind thought of Mr. Collins envisioning her father's demise and establishing himself in her home. Mr. Darcy reappeared at Elizabeth's side.

"What news have you learned, Miss Bennet?" Mr. Darcy asked. "Mr. Collins looked quite flustered and you look unwell."

Elizabeth threw Mr. Darcy a look of annoyance. As he had already caused enough damage in her family's life, she did not feel it was necessary for her to share with him the news she had recently received.

"It was a personal family matter," she told him. "I find myself unable to discuss it. Unfortunately I will also not be able to continue our conversation as I have urgent matters that require my attention. I shall be returning to Longbourn this evening."

"I understand." Mr. Darcy's face fell, but he regained his composure quickly. "But before I take my leave, you should know that I am not the man you think I am. I *do* hope that one day you will see that." With that, he left her alone.

Elizabeth and Mr. Darcy parted ways, each lost in their own thoughts but it seemed they would not be parted for long.

Later in the afternoon, Elizabeth was rushing to the nearby shops in hopes of purchasing a book for her father—before the carriage was scheduled to pick her up—when she bumped into Mr. Darcy again.

Even though she had made it clear she was in no disposition for conversation, he insisted on speaking with her, his mind unable to find rest until he shared with her his thoughts.

"What I have to say is of great importance, Miss Bennet," he said. "I do not feel, in good conscience, it can wait."

"And you found it best to follow me? Following young ladies is beneath a man of your stature, do you not think?" Elizabeth sighed. "I apologize that I am in no mood for conversation, Mr. Darcy. I should really be leaving." She gave him a brief nod. "I wish you a good day."

As Elizabeth walked away, she heard him say something to her, but the words were swallowed by the sounds of the market. It was just as well because her thoughts were captured with worry for her father.

CHAPTER 2

Upon arriving in Longbourn, Elizabeth stepped off the carriage before it came to a full halt, almost tripping on her dress.

She rushed into the house, her heart lodged in her throat. She could not imagine what she would do if something happened to Papa. He was everything to her. Of all the relationships he had with his other daughters, Elizabeth always felt theirs was the closest. In fact, she considered him to be her best friend, after Jane, of course.

The door was flung open before she got to it and her mother, Mrs. Bennet, filled the doorway, her arms open wide.

Elizabeth was taken aback momentarily. She could not understand why her mother would carry a smile on her face during such a difficult time. She had expected tears and hysterics.

"Lizzy, I am so glad you came back home." Mrs. Bennet's face was beaming.

"Of course, Mama, how could I stay away?" Still confused, Elizabeth allowed herself to be engulfed into an embrace by her mother, but she kept their contact brief. She had never been as warm to her mother as she was to her Papa. Since she was a little girl, her mother had a way of pushing her away without even trying.

"Where is he? Where's Papa?" she asked, pushing past the eldest female Bennet. "I would like to see him."

"Of course, of course, you do." Something in her mother's voice sounded off, but Elizabeth did not have time to wonder why.

"Lizzy," Jane appeared in front of her and pulled her into a hug. Elizabeth felt tears burn the backs of her eyes as she held on to her sister. Her vision was blurred when she broke the embrace. "What happened to Papa? Where is he?"

"He is in his study," Jane said, taking Elizabeth's hand. "I am certain he'll be happy to see you." Jane glanced at their mother, who soon disappeared into the kitchen to get tea.

Elizabeth rushed to Mr. Bennet's office, where she found her father sitting in his favourite chair, a newspaper on his lap, his eyes closed.

She dropped to her knees in front of him, tears welling up in her eyes. "Papa, are you all right? I am here."

It did surprise Elizabeth not to find her father in bed. From what Mr. Collins had said, she had expected him to be in a terrible state.

Mr. Bennet opened his eyes and a wide smile spread across his face when he saw her. "My darling Elizabeth, am I glad to see you. I did not hear you come in."

Elizabeth tipped her head to the side, studying his face. "You look well," she said with a frown, reaching for his hands.

"That's because I am. I am as strong as a horse. Why do you look so worried, my dear girl?"

"Papa, you wrote a letter to Mr. Collins asking for me to return to Longbourn because you were gravely ill."

Her father placed a hand on his

forehead. "I apologize, Elizabeth. The letter was written by your mother and signed by myself. I am afraid I had not read it. You know how she is."

Elizabeth pulled herself to her feet, still confused about what was going on. "Does that mean you're not ill at all?"

"I have not been this healthy in years." Mr. Bennet folded up the paper and placed it on the table next to the chair.

"I do not understand. Why would Mama claim you're ill when you're the picture of health?"

Mr. Bennet pinched the bridge of his nose. "I think it is best for her to explain it to you."

At that moment, Mrs. Bennet rushed into the room with steaming tea for Elizabeth and Mr. Bennet.

Elizabeth declined the cup of tea and took a seat. "Mama, Papa just told me you were the one who wrote the letter to Mr. Collins." She inhaled sharply. "You said Papa was very ill and I should return home at once." She glanced at her father. "He looks well enough to me. What reason should you have to end my visit with a friend so prematurely?"

Mrs. Bennet returned the tea she had offered Elizabeth back to the tray, her cheeks flushed. "You are correct. But Lizzy, you will soon understand why I did what I did. It was a matter of urgency."

"What was so urgent that you would tell an untruth about Papa's health?" Elizabeth's heart raced with each word.

Behind her mother, she spotted Jane standing in the doorway. She looked uncomfortable as she twirled a loose tendril of her honey blonde hair around her finger. Did she know what their mother had been up to?

Unable to face any more of her mother's schemes, Elizabeth was determined to find the answers in her sister. So she stood up and went to take Jane's hand, holding onto it until they were outside in the sunshine.

For a while, they walked without saying a word to each other while Elizabeth thought of how tortured she had been on the journey back home. She had dreaded seeing her father again, afraid she would find him in a condition much worse than Mr. Collins had said. And now here she was to find it was all a ploy to get her back. The question was, why?

Once they reached the stables, Elizabeth pulled Jane to a stop and turned to her. "I do not understand. Why would mother do such a thing?"

"I am sorry, Lizzy." Jane tightened her hand around Elizabeth's. "I had begged mother not to do it. She promised me she would not, and only told me after she had sent off the letter that she did it anyway."

"Why did she want me back so desperately? And why would she make a joke of Papa's health?"

Jane hesitated. "Dear Elizabeth, I am not sure whether her reasons would please or irritate you."

Elizabeth frowned. "And what are those reasons?"

Before Jane could reply, their mother's shrill voice reached them and they both turned to see her running towards them, her skirt bellowing in the wind. "He came," she breathed. "He is here. Elizabeth, you have to come inside at once."

Elizabeth glanced at Jane, perplexed.

"What's going on here?"

"I predict you're about to find out our mother's reasons for wanting you back."

Mrs. Bennet gripped Elizabeth's arm and very nearly forced her back into the house through the kitchen door. She did not release her until they were inside Elizabeth and Jane's bedroom, where she fussed with her daughter's hair.

"What's going on, mother?" Elizabeth asked, confused about her behavior.

Mrs. Bennet ran a brush through Elizabeth's locks. "A lady should look presentable at all times. You never know who you might meet."

"Please stop, Mama." Elizabeth stepped away. "I need to know what you have planned."

"I understand why you're upset, but someone else can explain my reasons better." Mrs. Bennet placed both hands on Elizabeth's cheeks. "You will understand shortly, my dear, why I had to do it."

"Oh, mother, you were the one who wrote the letter. I would prefer you explain this. I can think of no reason for such schemes."

"My dear Elizabeth, I assure you that you will be very appreciative of the reason. Come with me back to the drawing room and I will show you."

Before Elizabeth could further press for answers, her mother dragged her to the drawing room, where a handsome man with jet black hair and a matching moustache sat in a chair opposite her father. He looked strangely familiar, but she had no idea where she had seen him before.

When he saw her enter the room, he rose to his feet, a pleasant smile turning up the corners of his lips. When Jane came to stand next to Elizabeth, Elizabeth whispered into her ear. "Who is that?"

"Lizzy, allow me to introduce you to Prince Gabriel," Mrs. Bennet answered, clutching her hands together with excitement, her cheeks glowing. "He is a wealthy French prince, you see. And he traveled all the way from France to come and see you."

The prince chuckled as he approached Elizabeth and took one of her hands to press a kiss onto her skin.

"Miss Bennet, it is such a delight to see you again."

Elizabeth swallowed hard. "It is a pleasure, Prince... Gabriel?" she said hesitantly.

He had the most enchanting emerald eyes she had ever seen. As she continued to study his face, she wondered where she had seen him. He certainly had the kind of eyes no one would forget. "I fear you have me at a loss, sir. Have we met before?"

"Indeed, we have though I am not surprised that you do not remember." He let go of Elizabeth's hand.

"I apologize for my loss of memory. I had traveled in haste, fearing for my father's health." Elizabeth threw her mother a disapproving look, but nothing would censure Mrs. Bennet's good mood.

"We should leave you two alone to get reacquainted with one another." Mrs. Bennet crossed the room and pulled Mr. Bennet from his chair, then lured him and Jane out of the drawing room. She left the door open a modest yet appropriate amount, and Elizabeth could guess why.

Left alone, Elizabeth asked the prince to

return to his seat, her mind still running wild. "What brings you to England, Your Royal Highness?"

His lips curved into a smile. "England happens to be one of my favourite places to be."

"It is a beautiful country." Elizabeth returned his smile. "You spoke that we've met before. Would you mind refreshing my memory?"

"Yes, of course." Prince Gabriel rested his hands on his knees. "We met at the Meryton Ball. We exchanged a few words, but I could see that your mind was not present. Though, at the ball, none knew of my true stature."

Elizabeth sat down in her father's chair as she tried to remember the night she met Mr. Darcy, the night he began to occupy her mind against her will. Suddenly, she remembered a handsome man speaking with her, clearly seeking her attention. It was Prince Gabriel and she had inadvertently dismissed him, too busy being distracted by Mr. Darcy to pay the other man much heed. He had not mentioned to her then that he was a

French prince. But would that have made any difference to her, as riled as she'd been?

"I had asked you for a dance, remember?" he continued.

Elizabeth hung her head in shame. "I remember who you are now." She raised her eyes again to look at him. "I apologize if I treated you unkindly. I do not know what had come over me."

As she watched him, Elizabeth understood everything. She understood why her mother had desired her immediate return. Her dear mother was at it again, trying desperately to marry her and Jane off, her two unmarried oldest daughters. Lydia had married Mr. Wickham after they eloped, and Mary was married to Mr. Sutton, a successful London lawyer. Kitty—who was currently visiting Lydia in Cambridge—was the only other unmarried sister, but was safe from their mother's machinations only through her current distance.

It still upset Elizabeth to think her mother would use her father to ensure she returned to Longbourn. She would have preferred her to simply tell the truth. Perhaps she supposed Elizabeth would not be impressed by a prince. And she was right. She had quite enjoyed spending time with Charlotte in her new home. She had hoped to stay at least another week, despite Mr. Collin's boorish nature.

"Certainly you did not return to England simply to call on my company?" Elizabeth asked Prince Gabriel.

"Indeed, Miss Elizabeth, that is the exact reason for my return to the country. I was hoping you would give me the opportunity to dance with you in the near future." His green eyes lit up. Elizabeth couldn't help thinking he had a very arresting face—sculptured and strong, and such kind eyes.

"I have to say I am flattered." She found herself giggling like a little girl even though it was quite unlike her. She pressed the tips of her fingers to her lips, as if to stop the sound from escaping.

"I am glad I have finally caught your attention. I enjoyed watching you at the ball. You stood out from the rest of the ladies present." As he spoke, Elizabeth noticed that he spoke English fluently, with barely a hint of an accent.

"In what way?" Elizabeth was unable to wipe the smile off her face. She had never met such a charming man.

"Miss Bennet, I was close enough to hear the way you spoke. You were confident and unlike the other ladies, you did not seem desperate to catch a man's attention. I found that quite endearing about you."

"Are you telling me that desperate women do not appeal to you?" Elizabeth teased.

The prince chuckled and rubbed his moustache. "All I can say is that when I returned back to France, I found I could not forget your face. I had to come back to see if you would give me another chance to at least converse with you. When I arrived, and found that you were not in town, I was rather disappointed and thought perhaps it was not meant to be. But your dear mother assured me you planned to return to Longbourn soon and I should not lose heart."

"It would appear my mother is always

right." Elizabeth smiled in spite of herself.

"It appears she is." He leaned forward. "I am staying a few more days in Meryton and I would very much appreciate the chance to get better acquainted with you. What do you say?"

Elizabeth pulled in a breath and released it slowly. "Unfortunately, Prince Gabriel, I cannot provide you an answer right away. I am certainly flattered by your visit, and do not discourage you from calling upon me at a later date."

The man nodded and pushed himself to his feet. "In that case, I shall return another day for your answer. I will look forward to a favourable response." He kissed Elizabeth's hand again, and soon took his leave.

CHAPTER 3

❦

Elizabeth watched through the window as the prince's carriage pulled away from her home while Mrs. Bennet waved her silken handkerchief manically. Even from a distance, Elizabeth could see her mother's chest rising and falling with excitement. She would soon come to the drawing room to question her on her conversation with the prince. Truly, the world knew no better interrogator than her mother.

Elizabeth sighed deeply, regretting the error of her ways. She should not have treated the prince the way she had at the ball, being ignorant of his status offered no excuse. Unlike Mr. Darcy, he appeared so much more agreeable. And as though that were not enough, he seemed intelligent and apparently well-traveled. A few moments of talking to him were sufficient enough to show her that he was the complete opposite of Mr. Darcy.

She had willed herself to give him the answer he had wished for, but even though he had made a good impression on her, she felt that there was something still missing, something she was not able to put her finger on.

Before Elizabeth could work out her thoughts and emotions, Mrs. Bennet hurried into the drawing room followed closely by an amused Mr. Bennet.

"Do tell us, Lizzy," she cried, bringing her hands together. "Do not keep us in suspense. What did the prince say? Am I to be the mother-in-law to royalty? Lady Lucas would be quite envious!"

Elizabeth shook her head in amazement. "Mama, I am certain you heard every word he spoke to me. Why must I repeat them for you?"

"Oh, Elizabeth," Mrs. Bennet blushed, "I could not help myself."

"You never can," Mr. Bennet said with a dry chuckle, returning to his newspaper.

"Go on," Mrs. Bennet pushed, ignoring

Mr. Bennet. "It could be that I missed something."

Elizabeth was not surprised that her mother had taken to the prince. He was not only wealthy, but came from the royal family. He was certainly a most desirable suitor for one of her daughters; in fact, Elizabeth was certain that, were her mother not wed to her father, Mrs. Bennet would do her best to arrange her own marriage to the man.

"Mother, I am still quite cross with you forcing my return with such deception. Would it not have been easier for you to simply tell me I had a visitor in town?"

Her mother shrugged, clearly unapologetic. "Perhaps, but I was not certain you would return if I had been truthful. And if there is one thing I know about you, Elizabeth, it is that your father is very dear to you. I knew that once you heard he was ill, you would not hesitate to return."

Mr. Bennet had returned to his favourite chair and sat down to watch them in silence, the paper spread before him. Elizabeth wished he would say more, that he would make her mother aware of her wrongdoings.

"Mama, Elizabeth is right," Jane said, appearing in the room. "I had cautioned you against sending the letter."

"I had no choice." Mrs. Bennet glanced at both her daughters in irritation. "This is your best chance, Elizabeth." Desperate for her second-eldest daughter to understand, she went to clutch Elizabeth's arms. "You should give the prince an answer as soon as possible before he loses interest. He is a prince, my girl. I do not believe you could do any better. You would be royalty and the envy of even London society."

If there was one thing Elizabeth knew about her mother, it was that she would never change. It was best for them all to simply accept her. "Are you that afraid Jane and I will end up spinsters?"

"Do not play silly games, Elizabeth," Mrs. Bennet said in a clipped voice. "Go on, tell us what you have decided. The man has made an effort to come all this way to speak to you. In all the years I have lived, I have never seen a stronger gesture of affection."

"One thing I can tell you, mother, is that I *do* regret how I had acted at the Meryton Ball. I should have given him more of an opportunity to speak to me. But I will not allow anyone to push me into a marriage that I do not embrace, not even you, Mama."

"Good for you, Elizabeth," Mr. Bennet said finally, concealing his face with his newspaper. "The decision is yours and yours alone."

"Mr. Bennet, you've no care for my nerves. Be so kind as not to influence her decision. Elizabeth has much to consider, and I pray she will make the right choice of husband. Certainly she would not make the same mistake twice."

"I am very confident of that, my dear," Mr. Bennet said and leaned back in his chair to continue reading.

Mrs. Bennet continued her discourse to Mr. Bennet even though he did not look like he was listening. "Lizzy has already turned down Mr. Collins's proposal. Surely she would not allow another suitor to pass her by." She turned to look at Jane and

Elizabeth again. "Two of your younger sisters have already found husbands and you're still at home. What would people say if they heard you refused another proposal?"

Elizabeth moved to the window. "It is none of my concern what people say, Mama. As Papa mentioned, I shall make the choice that's right for me."

"And what choice would that be?" Mrs. Bennet folded her arms across her chest. "Tell me you will give the prince a chance. At least allow him to call upon you again."

Pushed into a corner, Elizabeth made a quick decision and turned to her mother with a small smile. "Yes, I will, Mama. I will give the prince a chance to call upon me."

"Oh, Elizabeth, that is wonderful news." Mrs. Bennet was so excited by the news that she moved around the room, touching one object after the other, picking up vases and ornaments before putting them back into place. "My daughter is marrying a prince. Can you imagine how lavish the wedding will be?"

Elizabeth laughed out loud. "Do not get

ahead of yourself, mother, the prince has yet to ask for my hand in marriage."

"I am certain he will make you an offer." Mrs. Bennet's eyes shone with unshed tears of joy. "How could he not? You are quite a beautiful woman."

Mr. Bennet chuckled. "Dare I assume that you have already started planning the wedding, Mrs. Bennet?"

Everyone in the room laughed except for Mrs. Bennet, whose face was tight with annoyance. She mumbled to herself as she straightened out the books on a shelf nearest to her.

Elizabeth and Jane could not hide their giggles. They both knew their father was right. Inside their mother's head, the wedding was already happening, whether the prince had proposed yet or not.

Elizabeth walked up to Jane and reached for her hand. "Can I have a word?" The two sisters walked out of the room and went to their shared bedroom.

"Are you absolutely certain this is what you want, Lizzy?" Jane asked the moment the door closed behind them.

"Mother was right about one thing,"

Elizabeth replied. "Prince Gabriel has made an effort in coming to see me. The least I can do is be polite."

"What of Mr. Darcy?" Jane's eyes searched Elizabeth's face for the truth. Elizabeth had often complained to her about the conflicting emotions Mr. Darcy had aroused in her. As much as Elizabeth had insisted that she was not taken with Mr. Darcy, Jane disagreed. She was of the opinion that since Elizabeth had been unable to stop talking about him, there was something more there.

"What do you mean?" Elizabeth asked. Now that she learned the truth of Mr. Darcy's character, she could not even bear the thought of him.

Jane lowered herself onto the bed. "I still feel you are drawn to him in some way."

"Jane, I find the man despicable. Even more so now that I discovered who he really is when I visited Charlotte. And beyond that, he has very little respect for our family. At least I think so of him." Elizabeth had resolved that she would not tell her sister of Mr. Darcy's role in Mr.

Bingley's decision to not pursue Jane. There was no use in upsetting her.

"Did you get a chance to speak to him?" Jane asked.

"I did, briefly." Elizabeth paused. "He had wished to speak to me about something he claimed to be of great importance, but Mr. Collins interrupted us with Mama's letter."

"What is it you think that he wished to discuss with you?"

Elizabeth shrugged. "It does not matter what he wanted to say, I had little desire to hear it. I wish to never cross paths with the man again. There is nothing he can say to me that would change my opinion of him."

"The prince it is, then?" Jane folded her hands in her lap, her face bright with excitement. "I did not have the pleasure of conversing much with him, but he seems to be a good man. And you have never been abroad. This might be a chance to see the world."

Elizabeth sat down next to Jane. "You are right. He is so different from any man I have ever known."

"I am truly excited for you, Lizzy." Jane

pulled Elizabeth into a warm embrace.

Although Jane was the eldest sister now with no suitor of her own, she knew no jealousy when it came to her sisters. Secretly she was still nursing her broken heart after Mr. Bingley let her down, but seeing Elizabeth find happiness made her just as happy.

Jane broke the embrace, but kept her hands on Elizabeth's shoulders. "If he proposes and you accept, do you think he would invite you to live in France?"

"Perhaps. I do not know if I would wish to live so far away from all of you."

"But why not? It would be your opportunity to live in another country. And we would certainly visit." Jane laughed. "I assure you mother would be a frequent visitor."

"I am sure of that." The two sisters laughed loudly and the sound brought their mother to the room. She opened the door and looked at both of them sternly.

"What are you two going on about?" she asked.

"We were speaking about Prince Gabriel," Jane said and shared a secret glance with Elizabeth.

"There is nothing to laugh about the prince. He was a complete gentleman. And he will make a good husband for you, Elizabeth." Mrs. Bennet pointed a finger at Elizabeth.

"And you know that for sure, mother, even though you have not known him for long?" Elizabeth teased.

"I am a very good judge of character." Mrs. Bennet planted her hands on her hips. "I am sure he will be back soon to call upon you again. I suggest you make a good impression."

"Do not worry, Mama. I shall not embarrass us more than we already embarrass ourselves."

"You silly child. We are a decent family. There are far worse families out there. If we were not good enough, the prince would not even consider becoming one of us."

"Unfortunately, he has not had a chance to see our true colours." Elizabeth poked Jane in the side with her elbow. "I wonder what he would say if he has the chance to learn more about our family."

Elizabeth thought back to Mr. Darcy's words, the things he said to Colonel Fitzwilliam about their family. What if Prince Gabriel came to the same conclusion once he got a chance to know them better? What if he decided she wouldn't be the right match for him after all? Certainly he would not want the Bennets to be an embarrassment to the royal family.

"Do not be foolish," Mrs. Bennet scolded her. "From this point on, we shall all be on our best behaviors."

Elizabeth said no more and instead chose to allow time to reveal what lay in store.

CHAPTER 4

Three days after Elizabeth arrived back at Longbourn, she agreed to go to Meryton to buy a new bonnet for Mrs. Bennet. But as she was leaving the house, Prince Gabriel arrived and offered to accompany her, claiming they had plenty to talk about. He had already come to visit two nights ago, and Elizabeth had given him her agreement.

As she had expected, he had been overjoyed for the opportunity to spend more time with her. But even though Elizabeth felt she had made the right decision, she was unable to shake the feeling that, though he seemed perfect, there was still something amiss.

"Lizzy, there is no longer a need for you to get the bonnet for me," Mrs. Bennet said quickly upon seeing the prince, unable to take her eyes off him. "I shall get one of the staff to do it. But *do* go on to Meryton, the both of you. I am certain you will find something to occupy you."

"A splendid idea," Prince Gabriel said and Elizabeth nodded. "You can show me around, Miss Bennet. In my previous travels, I was not afforded much time to explore."

"Excellent." Mrs. Bennet beamed. "Please, do not hurry back." She was clearly pleased that Elizabeth was spending more time with the prince. Every time Elizabeth talked to the prince, Mrs. Bennet pestered her about whether he had asked for her hand in marriage yet.

"But, Mama, it is really no bother. I can still stop by the milliner's shop to get the bonnet for you."

"Nonsense," Mrs. Bonnet scolded. "The prince deserves your complete attention." She placed a hand on Elizabeth's back, pushing her towards Prince Gabriel. "Go and enjoy yourself in Meryton."

"Are you sure this is what you want?" Elizabeth asked Prince Gabriel when Mrs.

Bennet disappeared into the house.

"I would go anywhere with you, Miss Bennet. In fact, I look forward to seeing more of your town. With you by my side, it would be that much more enjoyable."

"In that case, I would appreciate the company." Elizabeth allowed the prince to take her arm and help her into the carriage.

Several minutes later, Prince Gabriel and Elizabeth were enjoying their stroll around Meryton, with Elizabeth showing him all the things she had grown up seeing. Although there was much to see, the prince only had eyes for her.

"What do you think of my family?" She couldn't help asking when they stopped for refreshments at the newest tea shop in Meryton.

"I find them quite amusing," he replied.

Elizabeth nodded. "In a good or unpleasant way?"

"Certainly in a good way." His eyes crinkled at the corners as he smiled. "In all honesty, I find your family rather refreshing compared to mine. I grew up with too many rules and restrictions. It is refreshing to be able to relax instead of worrying that I'd be breaking some kind of rule or other."

Elizabeth had not expected his response at all. She had still been worried that he would be put off by her mother and her overenthusiasm in bringing them together. But the genuine look on his face gave her no reason to doubt his words.

"Can you tell me more about your family?" She sipped her tea. "Do you have siblings?"

"There's not much to tell really. But yes, I do have an older sister. Also, while my father is French, my mother is actually English."

"No wonder you speak English so fluently and with barely an accent."

"My mother made certain she spoke English to us from a very young age. She did not want us to lose sight of our roots here. And we visited England often, when we were not visiting another country."

"That's fascinating," Elizabeth said that he had been so blessed to have the opportunity to travel. "Do you prefer living in France or England?"

The prince rubbed his brow. "I have to

say I am drawn to both places. It depends on the season of the year, I guess."

Elizabeth nodded. "It must be lovely to be able to chase good weather. I have never been abroad, nor has anyone in my family."

"We will have to change that sometime. You will have to come to France."

The intensity with which he looked at Elizabeth brought out the shyness in her which caused her to lower her gaze. "I am sure France is a beautiful country. I have read much about it. Perhaps one day I will go there."

"That day need not be too far off." Prince Gabriel touched Elizabeth's hand briefly. "Miss Bennet, I have been having a wonderful time with you and your family." He paused. "When I returned to France after the Meryton Ball, you were all I could think about. Even though at the time I had been promised to another."

"You broke off the engagement?" Elizabeth's eyes widened and something fluttered in the pit of her stomach.

"I couldn't possibly marry someone else when my thoughts were captured by another. I value honesty above all else. And I am a true believer in the fact that one should enter into a marriage with a person they feel the most affection for."

"I fully agree," Elizabeth said, averting her gaze. For some reason, she was unable to look him in the eye. She was certainly drawn to him, yet there was still that nagging voice in her head that tried to discourage her from letting him in fully.

They continued their conversation throughout the day as they walked down the streets of Meryton. Along the way, a little girl who worked as a flower vendor entered their path, her face smeared with dirt and her hair resembling a bird's nest. But the roses in her basket were clean and fresh, and their sweet, untainted scent rose into the air.

"A flower for the lady?" The girl picked one flower from the basket and handed it to the prince.

Not wanting to embarrass him, Elizabeth shook her head quickly. "You do not need to."

"Of course, I do." Prince Gabriel cut Elizabeth off and beamed at the girl. "Tell you what, I will take the entire basket. This lady deserves a full garden of roses."

The girl pushed the basket into his hands quicker than Elizabeth could digest Prince Gabriel's words and grabbed the coins he handed her quickly. Then she rushed off before the prince could change his mind.

"You did not have to do that, Prince Gabriel." It was unusual for Elizabeth to be showered with gifts by a suitor. Since being in town, he had already gifted her books, chocolates from France, and had even bought gifts for her parents. Elizabeth feared that the more she took from him, the more she would be required to give back. And at this point, she was still unsure of what her response to a possible proposal would be.

"My dear Miss Bennet, flowers this beautiful belong with an equally beautiful woman." He handed her the basket and she felt her cheeks colour.

"Thank you, Mr. Darcy," she said as her fingers wrapped around the woven handle. When she caught sight of the confused look on Prince Gabriel's face, she realized what she had just said. Her cheeks warmed with humiliation as she put on a trembling smile. "I apologize. I meant to say Prince... Prince Gabriel."

Prince Gabriel still had on a puzzled expression. "Is Mr. Darcy one of the men who had been present at the ball? I seem to remember his name mentioned."

Elizabeth shifted from one foot to the other. "He is nothing more than an unfortunate acquaintance." To distract him from the conversation, she took his arm and they continued to walk. "Come with me. I would like to show you the gallery."

She was relieved when Prince Gabriel no longer pursued the topic and they had a splendid time together at the gallery. But as they were about to leave, Elizabeth thought she saw Mr. Darcy strolling through the gallery, admiring the paintings.

She shook her head to clear it. Her mind had to be playing tricks on her. What was the matter with her? First, she said his name without thinking and now she was seeing him. Of course Mr. Darcy was not in town. Surely someone would have mentioned it if he were. He had left a firm impression on the citizens of Meryton.

She tried not to give him any more thought as they headed to the milliner's shop. But the same thing happened again. She thought she saw Mr. Darcy entering the shop after they walked in. Her heart unsettled, Elizabeth stopped walking and looked around, perplexed, but she could no longer see him.

"Are you all right, Miss Eliza?" Prince Gabriel asked, taking the basket from her. "This must be too heavy for you."

"Yes, yes, I am quite fine." Elizabeth swallowed hard. "Thank you. The basket was heavy."

"Do you feel unwell?" The prince placed a hand on her lower arm. His hand felt too warm against her skin.

Elizabeth shook her head and lifted her chin. "I am perfectly all right. You are very kind to be concerned about my wellbeing."

During the time they spent in the milliner's shop, Elizabeth found herself becoming more drawn to the prince, especially when she discovered—through their long conversation—that he shared the love for books that she, too, enjoyed.

Elizabeth had always dreamt of marrying someone who loved reading as much as she did and Prince Gabriel was making every one of her dreams a reality.

"I had a wonderful day," Prince Gabriel said when they finally returned to the carriage. "I will not forget the time I spent in your presence."

"I had a lovely time as well." Elizabeth paused. "Thank you for the flowers. They are beautiful."

"So are you," he said, his voice lowered to a whisper.

Before they arrived at the Longbourn house, it started to rain. Elizabeth stared out of the carriage window as beautiful nature blurred by. She was unable to enjoy it fully as she wondered whether she really *did* see Mr. Darcy earlier that day. She pulled herself together quickly as it was impolite to think of another man while she was with the prince.

"Miss Elizabeth Bennet," Prince Gabriel said minutes before they arrived at the house. "I have been watching you the past days and I have enjoyed your company." He waited for her to face him before continuing. "There is no doubt in my mind that we would share many more wonderful moments together. Therefore, I have decided to stay longer in town in order to see where this journey would lead us. I hope to one day have the opportunity to show you my country of France and introduce you to my family."

Elizabeth did not have to force her lips into a smile. "I have enjoyed your company as well, Prince Gabriel. It has filled me with much pleasure to learn of our similar passions. If your country and family are even at least half as wonderful as your company, I would find myself blessed to know them. I would look favourably upon your company again."

As soon as the carriage arrived, Elizabeth said goodbye to the prince as he was unable to come into the house, much to Mrs. Bennet's disappointment when Elizabeth told her. He had business to take care of at the inn and he would return in the morning to see Elizabeth. She perked up when Elizabeth told her that he planned on extending his stay.

Elizabeth went to bed feeling both

excited and uneasy. Her excitement at finally finding a suitable suitor was overshadowed by clouds of doubt. She could not understand where they were coming from when the prince was so perfect.

It irritated her that Mr. Darcy appeared in her thoughts during her time with the prince when he was the last person she desired to think about.

As she closed her eyes to fall asleep, she banished the images of him from her mind and forced herself to think of Prince Gabriel instead.

CHAPTER 5

∾

Mr. Darcy sat inside the carriage that had brought him to Meryton, watching Elizabeth Bennet drive away in another carriage, accompanied by someone else.

Elizabeth had been right when she told him in Kent that it was beneath him to pursue a gentleman's daughter in the way he had.

But when she left so suddenly, Mr. Darcy had been unable to stop himself from following her to Hertfordshire. After witnessing the pained look on her face the last time he saw her, he could not bear it if he remained in Kent when he could offer his assistance and ease her pain.

When he had arrived in Hertfordshire, he was determined to call at Longbourn house at once, but after hearing rumors of a suitor of great stature in town to win Elizabeth's hand in marriage, he hesitated.

As soon as the rumors reached him, several days ago, he did not have the courage to show his face outside the walls of Netherfield, where he was staying.

It was not only Mr. Darcy who had returned to Hertfordshire. When he had voiced his plans to Mr. Bingley, his friend had offered to join him and offer him residence at Netherfield Park, where Mr. Darcy stayed out of sight.

Mr. Darcy knew he could not hide for long. His heart demanded he find out if the rumors had any truth to them.

Now that he knew that Elizabeth Bennet was indeed the focus of another man's affections, and she appeared to encourage them, it pained him deeply that he had wasted the chance to tell her of his own love. And when he learned that her suitor was not just any gentleman, but a prince from France, he felt certain it was too late for his own happiness.

For although he was a man of great wealth, how could he possibly compete with someone from royal blood? Even from a distance, Mr. Darcy could see that the prince was a handsome man and he carried himself in a way that showed confidence and grace.

When he caught sight of them in Meryton, he had been unable to stay away from the pair, desperate to see more of Elizabeth. It was completely out of his character to act in such a manner, but he was driven by something stronger than himself, something he had never experienced before. Although he hesitated to put the feeling into words, he knew what it was.

That feeling had driven him to follow them into the gallery while he made sure to keep a safe distance, staying in the shadows so they would not notice him. He suspected at one point that Elizabeth might have seen him, but she couldn't have or else her character would have driven her to confront him. It would have been common courtesy necessitated by society as well. Unfortunately he had been unable to bring himself to approach them. He knew she would not be amused to find him in Meryton.

Mr. Darcy had watched as she leaned into the prince as though they had been acquainted for quite some time. Was he the reason for her return? He must mean something to Elizabeth for her to cut her plans short in order to come and see him. But why had she looked so upset? He hated to think that her source of misery could possibly lie with him and not the news Mr. Collins had shared with her. The usually over-verbose Mr. Collins had been quite silent on the correspondence when he had asked.

Mr. Darcy leaned back in his seat and closed his eyes as he remembered the way his chest had tightened when Elizabeth had thrown her head back to laugh at something the prince had said to her. The brilliance of her laughter had drifted all the way to Mr. Darcy's ears, torturing him.

She had never laughed like that in his presence. The only thing he was accustomed to was the slow, sometimes sarcastic smile she seemed to hold in sole reservation for him. He couldn't imagine ever making her laugh the way the prince had. The laughter he brought out of her was light and untainted by life's troubles, like that of an innocent child.

Mr. Darcy hated to think that if the prince proposed to Elizabeth and she accepted, he would spirit her away with him to France. From what he had observed, the two clearly enjoyed each other's company. They appreciated the same art as they stood in front of the paintings, discussing them for longer than Mr. Darcy found it necessary to admire a painting. Although he appreciated art himself, and had an extensive gallery of his own in his beloved Pemberley, it was unlike him to spend hours on end admiring the artwork.

As he watched them, he struggled with the urge to approach them, to speak to Elizabeth and tell her once and for all what was on his mind; the things he had been unable to say before Mr. Collins had interrupted them.

He deeply regretted the things he had said about her family. The more he saw her with the prince, the less he cared about the behavior of her mother and younger sisters. All he cared about was the real fear of losing her affections to another man.

Every time Elizabeth and the prince walked away from a painting that had held their attention, he had moved to it to try and understand what she saw in the individual pieces of art, to learn her preferences. But it was hard to make out the paintings she was drawn to the most. She seemed to enjoy them all.

After they'd left the gallery, he had also followed them to the milliner's shop and at one point, he was close enough to hear the prince communicate his love for the same books she read, but also his feelings for her. He seemed desperate to win her heart.

Mr. Darcy opened his eyes and blew out a laboured breath, then he exited the carriage once more, not ready to drive off just yet.

Outside, he looked again in the direction the carriage in which Elizabeth rode had headed. It was no longer visible to his eyes.

Although he was surrounded by a large number of people, he had never felt more alone.

Finally, he stepped away from the carriage and returned to the gallery that

Elizabeth had visited earlier. He could not understand what pulled him back there, but he found himself walking inside again and studying the paintings.

He returned to every painting Elizabeth had admired until he came to the conclusion that the one she had spent the most time at—and perhaps loved the most—was one of a sad little girl sitting alone by a lake, gazing out into the horizon. Although the painting had no effect on Mr. Darcy, he fooled himself into believing he felt the same emotions Elizabeth had felt while admiring it.

She must have loved it so much because at one point the prince had called over the gallery owner. Mr. Darcy had speculated that perhaps he had been interested in purchasing it for Elizabeth. But she had gazed at the prince with a smile as she shook her head.

Secretly he hoped she refused because she was having doubts about becoming attached to the prince. But another part of his mind told him that perhaps the prince had already gifted her something far more valuable and she felt it was impolite to ask for more.

But maybe there was something Mr. Darcy could learn from the prince. After all, he was the one holding the key to Elizabeth's heart at the moment.

A frown formed between his eyebrows as he stood back to get a better look at the painting, as though he was searching for a divine answer within the colours.

He stood in front of the painting for such a long time that the gallery owner appeared to inquire whether he was interested in purchasing it.

Mr. Darcy shook his head without comment and moved on to another painting. Even though this particular painting also did nothing for him, an idea soon crossed his mind. Could it be he had discovered the key to Elizabeth's heart? Perhaps art was the answer, the one thing which could soften her heart so he could turn it in his favour.

Though she had another suitor, from what he learned, he had not yet made a proposal to her. Maybe Mr. Darcy still had a chance, after all. He had been a fool each time he had spoken to Elizabeth in the past, and this would be his final chance to make things right and convince her of the sincerity of his affections.

If he failed, he might never see her again if she decided to call France her new home. He had not expected the mere thought of losing her to devastate him as much as it did.

Mr. Darcy walked out of the gallery and made his way to his carriage. On the way, he came across a girl trying to sell him roses. He turned away from her, ignoring her calls and entered the carriage. But he continued to watch the flower girl as the carriage pulled away, remembering another girl from earlier who had sold an entire basket of roses to the prince which he had then gifted Elizabeth.

Mr. Darcy had never considered himself to be a romantic gentleman, and he did not understand how other men found it so easy to win a woman's heart. It would have never crossed his mind to buy an entire basket of flowers in a display of affection.

He certainly had a lot to learn. The days he already spent in Hertfordshire had already brought out parts of him he never knew existed, emotions he did not know he was capable of experiencing.

As his carriage moved along a dirt road, his mind continued to return to Elizabeth. He had to make haste in winning her heart before someone else won her away from him.

At the very least, he needed to say what was on his mind to allow Elizabeth to make a fair decision; to let her decide whether he was, in fact, the one for her or if she preferred to pursue happiness with the prince. He needed to show Elizabeth another side to him that she had not seen yet. Whether she would forgive him for the things he had said about her family, he could not say, but he would not forgive himself for not trying.

Mr. Darcy and Elizabeth may not seem from the outside to be similar, but he believed they were to some extent. For one, they both valued honesty and were not afraid to speak their minds. Even though they did not share an extensive love of similar artwork, at least they had that.

He strove to come up with more

similarities between them, but he found none. He could only think of their differences, both in personality and certainly in standings in society.

When he returned to Netherfield, he was still blinded by thoughts of Elizabeth, unable to forget her smile, her laughter, her face. He wanted more of what he saw in her today. He found her full of life, and he found that she was strong when she needed to be, but also gentle and feminine.

Today he had appreciated just how beautiful she was. That realization made him feel like a fool for what he had said to Mr. Bingley at the Meryton Ball, that Elizabeth was not handsome enough to tempt him. He had said then that the only beautiful woman in the room was Elizabeth's sister, Jane. But now he found himself mistaken. In fact, if he were asked the question again, he would choose Elizabeth even over her sister's fair appearance.

It had been her all along, even when he tried his best to deny it. His prejudice had blinded his eyes and shielded his heart.

When he entered through the doors of

Netherfield, he felt like a changed man, much different from the one who had gone to town that morning. And it was all because of Elizabeth Bennet.

CHAPTER 6

A day had passed since Mr. Darcy saw Elizabeth in Meryton, and he could not bring himself to walk the town streets, even though he was desperate to see her again, to talk to her. Instead of gathering his courage to return to the Longbourn house, he spent the day with Mr. Bingley.

It was a relief to Mr. Darcy that Mr. Bingley's sisters had not accompanied them to Hertfordshire. He could not bear to spend an extended period of time in their presence. Especially that of Caroline, who made no disguise of her interest in him.

Mr. Darcy and Mr. Bingley were both relaxing in the sitting room long after supper, drinking tea and reading the papers, and Mr. Darcy contemplated whether he should open up to his friend.

When Mr. Darcy had returned to Netherfield after seeing Elizabeth, Mr. Bingley had questioned him about his excursion, but Mr. Darcy had not been in the right mind to discuss it with him. But now, after a moment of hesitation, he decided he needed to unburden himself, putting into words his feelings for Elizabeth, especially the pain he felt at the idea of losing her.

"That rather surprises me," Mr. Bingley said when Mr. Darcy had revealed the nature of his turmoil. "I had the impression you did not think much of Elizabeth. In fact I believed you found her unattractive."

Mr. Darcy was not surprised by Mr. Bingley's confusion. Up to this moment, whatever Mr. Darcy had felt for Elizabeth, he had kept to himself. Even when Mr. Bingley had inquired into his reasons for returning to Hertfordshire, he had not mentioned Elizabeth's name once, simply saying it was a place he wished to see again.

"I was unsure of how I felt about Elizabeth, but I did not despise her. It was her family—her mother in particular—I was not fond of." Mr. Darcy pushed back his shoulders. "However, as time passed, I found myself being increasingly drawn to her." Mr. Darcy took another sip of tea, then decided to be completely honest with his most trusted friend. "My reason for visiting Meryton was in the hopes that I would see her again."

"And did you?" Mr. Bingley raised an eyebrow.

"I did, indeed," Mr. Darcy said. "Unfortunately she was on another gentleman's arm."

"Is that so?" Mr. Bingley leaned forward. "I never felt the need to mention this, but I did hear talk of a foreign prince coming to town to win her heart. So it is true then?"

"I am afraid so. I saw them with my own eyes. I have heard that they have been seen frequently in each other's company."

"Do not tell me you followed them." An amused smile appeared on Mr. Bingley's face.

"It had not been my intention. My foolish heart made me do it." Mr. Darcy hesitated, suddenly filled with shame. "I am ashamed to have stooped to a level so low, but I could not help myself. I feel bewitched by the woman."

"Did it yield any results, at least?" Mr. Bingley drank his tea, his eyes still on Mr. Darcy's face.

"I would like to think so. I have learned a thing or two about Elizabeth's interests. I discovered a softer side to her I had not yet had the chance to see." Mr. Darcy told Mr. Bingley everything he observed while in Meryton.

"In your opinion, did she seem happy?" Mr. Bingley asked when he heard the whole story.

"I cannot say for sure. Sometimes looks can be deceiving." Mr. Darcy was afraid to face the truth that Elizabeth could truly be happy with the prince. A truth he was not ready to accept yet, not until he got himself heard.

Mr. Bingley was silent for a long time, then he leaned forward. "My dear friend, it is clear to me that you're smitten with Miss Elizabeth Bennet. But what if it is too late?"

"What if it is not?" Mr. Darcy asked.

"What would you do to win her heart? I am assuming it would be a challenge to compete against a prince."

"That may be so. But I am certain I would regret it if I do not face the challenge." Mr. Darcy inhaled sharply. "While in the gallery, an idea came to me and I am thinking of pursuing it."

"What does the gallery have to do with you winning over Elizabeth?"

"I found that she was happiest when she was surrounded by art. I am thinking, perhaps, art is the key to her heart."

"So you intend on purchasing art for her?"

Mr. Darcy pinched the bridge of his nose. "I am not quite sure yet. But I will know what to do when the time is right. I shall figure something out."

"You're speaking as a true romantic." Mr. Bingley released a deep sigh and leaned back in his chair. "I applaud you, Darcy for taking on the challenge to win over the woman you love. Unlike myself, who never had the courage to keep the woman that touched my heart."

Mr. Darcy felt his heart sink. "You're speaking of Miss Jane Bennet, are you not?"

Mr. Bingley nodded. "I walked away without giving us a proper chance."

Mr. Bingley's response caused guilt to stab Mr. Darcy in the chest. "You still feel something for her?"

"I do. She was the most beautiful woman I have ever come across and her heart is as pure as her beauty." He put on a bittersweet smile. "Darcy, the reason I followed you here was because I wish to find my way back into her good graces and, hopefully, her life. If only I could be as romantic as you are."

Mr. Darcy laughed out loud, which was rare for him. "Me, a romantic?"

"Of course. You are most certainly more romantic than I could ever be. Your plan to reach Elizabeth through her love for art is impressive. Myself on the other hand, I have no plan to call my own, even though I cannot remove Jane from my mind. I try to ignore my feelings for her, but it is turning out to be an impossible task."

"I know I am partly to blame for your

heartache." Mr. Darcy brought his hands together. "I apologize for advising you to keep your distance from her and her family. I should not have interfered. If you choose to pursue a future with her again, I shall not stand in your way. Indeed, I would be required to encourage it, seeing as I seek my happiness with her sister."

"Do not be so hard on yourself, my friend. You were only looking out for me. At the time, I wasn't even sure what true affection for a woman felt like. It took the pain of losing her to make me realize I do not want to live without her. I pray it is not too late for me… or for you."

"I wish for the same," Mr. Darcy said.

Silence fell between the two men while each drowned in his own thoughts.

Mr. Darcy was the first to speak as he sat back and looked his friend straight in the eye. "Now that I know how it feels to have my heart stolen by a woman, I will never forgive myself for standing in your way. I am truly sorry."

Seeking forgiveness was yet another clue of the changes taking place within Mr. Darcy. He had always been of the belief that asking for forgiveness was a sign of weakness. And he liked to believe he was always right. He now realized that he had been wrong in so many ways. He had to make things right both with Mr. Bingley and with Elizabeth.

"Let us no longer focus on the past. We have much work ahead of us and we cannot afford any distractions." Mr. Bingley rubbed the back of his head. "And if we are honest, what happened between Jane and me was not entirely your fault. I should have been firm enough in my affections to fight for her, instead of giving up so easily."

"I appreciate your kind words, Bingley. I wish I could help you in finding your way back to her."

"The sentiment is appreciated, my friend, but this is something I might have to do alone. I will eventually find the courage to face her, to apologize for the way I had treated her by disappearing from her life the way I did with no prior warning." Mr. Bingley paused with a smile. "Now that you are drawn to Elizabeth Bennet, does that mean you have changed your feelings about her family?"

Mr. Darcy took a long moment to think, then he formed a steeple with his fingers, placing the tip underneath his chin. "Surprisingly, the Bennet family no longer seems to affect me as it once did before."

"That's good to hear," Mr. Bingley said.

"I agree. Now tell me, my friend, is there anything I can do to help make it easier for you to win over Jane?"

"That's kind of you, but I cannot think of anything at the moment. First, I must come up with the right words to say to her."

"Well, when you do decide what to do, I am ready to offer my assistance." A slow smile spread across Mr. Darcy's face. "Look at us, sitting here like two old men with broken hearts. Who would have thought we would both be pining for the Bennet sisters?"

Mr. Bingley joined his friend in laughter. "I rather enjoy this time together with you, Darcy. I feel like I can learn a thing or two from you."

Mr. Darcy laughed. "Be careful what you choose to learn from me. As you know from experience, sometimes I am not the person to take romantic advice from. But there is no better advice I can give you right now than to follow your heart."

"I intend on doing just that. Let us hope Jane has not moved on with another suitor, like your Elizabeth."

Mr. Darcy paused a moment to allow Mr. Bingley's words to sink in. *Your Elizabeth.* He liked the sound of that.

She was not yet *his* Elizabeth, but he intended on changing that, if luck was on his side. If he ended up failing, he knew that no other woman's love could penetrate his heart.

"I am afraid I must retire for the evening." Mr. Bingley yawned. "I had a long day of worrying behind me."

"So did I." Mr. Darcy chuckled. "And you are right. It is rather late. I have a busy day ahead of me tomorrow."

Mr. Bingley frowned. "Am I right in guessing you plan to pay Elizabeth a visit?"

Mr. Darcy nodded. "That's correct."

"Are you ready to face her?"

"If there's one thing I have learned about myself in the past days, it is that I do not handle regrets very well." Mr. Darcy rose from his seat. "I need to find out if I have a chance with her. If I ever had a chance."

"Good for you, Darcy. I wish you all the luck in the world."

Mr. Darcy and Mr. Bingley parted ways, each heading to their rooms. In his bed, Mr. Darcy spent many hours of the night thinking about the words he would say to Elizabeth when they came face to face again. Would tomorrow end with him walking away with a broken heart, or one filled with joy?

CHAPTER 7

Mr. Darcy dismounted from his horse, still determined to have a word with Elizabeth Bennet. He had come this far and would not allow anything or anyone to get in the way.

It was not Elizabeth who opened the door, but Mrs. Bennet and she did not look at all pleased to see him.

"Mr. Darcy," she said with a pinched expression, clearly forcing herself to be polite. "What brings you here this morning? I did hear from Lady Lucas that you're back in town, but I must say I did not expect you to call upon Longbourn."

Mr. Darcy neared the woman he hoped would one day become his mother-in-law. "Mrs. Bennet. It is a pleasure to see you again." He came to a halt in front of her.

"I had hoped to have a word with your daughter, Miss Elizabeth."

Mrs. Bennet gave him a tight smile. "I am afraid she is not in at the moment. She is rather busy these days."

"That's unfortunate." Mr. Darcy's chest tightened with disappointment. "Perhaps I may call upon Mr. Bennet, if he is not otherwise engaged?"

"Of course, Mr. Darcy." Mrs. Bennet's words sounded far from genuine, but she stepped aside to allow him entry into her home.

The interior of the Longbourn house was inviting, something the grand house Mr. Darcy grew up in never was. As a boy he had always felt it to be rather cold.

Even though he had said such unkind things about the Bennet family, he did appreciate their closeness. Perhaps that was the reason they had made him uneasy at the start. A family's closeness was something he was not accustomed to. If Elizabeth were to become his wife, he would have to change his views and embrace her family as his own.

Mrs. Bennet sent a maid to call upon her

husband and Mr. Darcy struggled to feel at ease with the woman since her pronouncement of Elizabeth's absence. But he was unable to overcome the feeling that she did not care for his presence. What would stop her from telling him an untruth to get him to leave? When the maid returned with news of Mr. Bennet's occupation, Mr. Darcy looked to the matron of Longbourn.

Mrs. Bennet, unable to be entirely inhospitable, showed him to the drawing room and offered him tea, which he accepted gratefully. Then she sat down in a chair that was quite a distance from him.

"Mr. Darcy, may I ask what you wish to speak to Elizabeth about?" she asked after a moment of tense silence.

Mr. Darcy took a drink of his tea for courage, watching Mrs. Bennet over the rim of his cup. "I am afraid it is of a personal nature." What he had to say was for Elizabeth's ears only. He did not wish Mrs. Bennet to distort his message when she shared it with Elizabeth.

Mrs. Bennet observed him for a long time, a clouded expression on her face. She did not approve of his response. But she forced a smile and clasped her hands in her lap. "Mr. Darcy, do you wish to tell me that you have found an interest in my daughter?"

"Mrs. Bennet, I would much rather discuss the reason for my visit with Elizabeth, if you do not mind. May I ask when she would return?"

"Unfortunately, I do not know. I expect her to be out for most of the day really." Mrs. Bennet suddenly got to her feet and started to fuss with the items around the room, straightening curtains and sofa pillows and removing a film of dust from the windowsill with the tip of her finger. When she turned to face Mr. Darcy again, her cheeks were flushed. "She is spending the day with her fiancé, the prince."

"Her fiancé." Mr. Darcy was taken aback for a moment. He did not like the sound of this. Was he too late? Had Elizabeth already decided?

"She is engaged to be married to a wonderful man, have you not heard?"

Mr. Darcy said nothing. It did not stop Mrs. Bennet from continuing. "Lizzy is very happy, and nothing will come in the way of her marriage to the prince." She snatched a breath. "He is a real prince from a foreign land."

"Yes, I had heard." Mr. Darcy mopped his forehead with a handkerchief. "People have spoken of him around town." It was hard for him to believe it was too late and he no longer had a chance. "Is she truly happy?" he asked to make sure.

Mrs. Bennet peered at him as though he was out of his mind. "Of course Elizabeth is happy. She is marrying a prince, a very wealthy and intelligent man. No one else is worthy of her hand."

Mr. Darcy nodded. "I find I must agree with you, Mrs. Bennet. No one is worthy of Elizabeth's hand in marriage, except the one she truly loves."

Mrs. Bennet lowered herself back into her seat. "Are you trying to be smart with me, Mr. Darcy?"

"Not at all, madam." Mr. Darcy adjusted his smile. "I am merely stating the facts."

Mrs. Bennet wagged a finger at him. "I may not have the accomplishments of other gentlewomen, young man, but I am no one's fool."

"She is certainly not anyone's fool," Mr. Bennet walked into the drawing room. "But, apparently, I am her fool."

"What are you trying to say, Mr. Bennet?" Mrs. Bennet shot him a look.

"Nothing, my dear, only that I was so blind that I did not see into your plot to lure Elizabeth back to Longbourn by making her believe I was unwell. I should have read the letter you sent Mr. Collins. Only a fool fails to do that, would you not agree?" He looked away from a fuming Mrs. Bennet and stretched his hand out to Mr. Darcy in greeting. "Mr. Darcy, what a pleasant surprise. It is a pleasure to see you again in our home. I apologize for my delay."

"It is my pleasure as well." Mr. Darcy shook his hand but was unable to get his words out of his head. "Is the letter you mentioned the one that was sent to Elizabeth in Kent?" Mr. Collins had mentioned to Mr. Darcy that he had received a letter from Longbourn which was why Elizabeth had left, but he had not shared the contents.

"As a matter of fact, that is the letter. My dear Mrs. Bennet wrote it in my name, claiming I was ill to ensure Elizabeth's swift return home. The fool that I was, I signed my name without reading it."

"What do you mean exactly?" Mr. Darcy asked, his interest piqued. He glanced at Mrs. Bennet who was unable to hide her annoyance. "May I ask why you wished her to return so suddenly, Mrs. Bennet? Do you not approve of her friendship with Mrs. Collins?"

Mrs. Bennet lifted her chin. "This is a family matter, Mr. Darcy."

"Oh, go on, Mrs. Bennet," Mr. Bennet chuckled. "Why not admit to him you wanted Elizabeth to come home and meet the prince?"

"Mr. Bennet, that's enough." Mrs. Bennet tried hard to keep her voice controlled, but she failed.

And the damage had already been done. This piece of news could change everything for Mr. Darcy. If Elizabeth did not willingly return to Longbourn, perhaps he still had a chance. It would have been more daunting a task if she had known the prince was waiting for her, and she could not wait to see him.

"Forget I said anything." Mr. Bennet waved a hand. "I'd rather not set my own wife against me. I am afraid I cannot stay, Mr. Darcy. I have some appointments in Meryton."

Mr. Bennet soon left and Mrs. Bennet did not waste time in getting Mr. Darcy to leave as well.

"I find my days filled with planning a wedding. I am certain you must have some idea of the extravagant nature a wedding to a man of royal blood would be. I find I hardly have the time to rest. It is fortunate that I have two daughters already wed."

"Of course, I do." Mr. Darcy pushed himself to his feet. "I have taken up too much of your time. I shall now take my leave."

Outside the house, Mr. Darcy was about to get into the carriage when he spotted Jane Bennet as she plucked flowers in the garden. Upon seeing him, she came to greet him.

"Mr. Darcy, how lovely to see you." She wore a smile that was much warmer than that of her mother's.

At seeing her kind face, Mr. Darcy felt a pang in his heart for having kept her from Mr. Bingley. Jane would make a fine wife for his friend. "How have you been, Miss Bennet?" he asked.

"Very well, thank you," she said, her smile widening. "Would you care to take a walk with me before you leave?"

"I'd like that very much." Mr. Darcy could see no reason to deny her invitation. Perhaps speaking with her would shed more light on what he had heard from Mrs. Bennet.

"I was not aware you were back in Hertfordshire. But then again, I do not frequent the town these days. Someone would have mentioned it there."

"Not many people know," Mr. Darcy said as he walked beside her, the morning sun warming the top of his head. "Your mother *did* know, though."

Mr. Darcy did not need to look behind him to know Mrs. Bennet was watching them from a distance.

"Really? She never said a word." Jane paused. "May I ask what drove you to call upon Longbourn?"

It did not surprise Jane that her mother had failed to mention her knowledge of Mr. Darcy's presence in town. She would do her best to keep any other potential suitor away from Elizabeth.

"I had wished to speak to your sister, Miss Elizabeth, but I have come at an inopportune time, it appears." He answered.

"That's right," Jane said. "She is in Meryton at the moment."

"I see," Mr. Darcy wished she would say more without him having to ask for additional information.

In companionable silence they made their way through Mrs. Bennet's rose garden, towards a small pond.

"I had the pleasure of seeing your sister in Kent. I had wished to speak further with her, but she rushed back home because of a family matter."

He turned to look at Jane just in time to see her pale cheeks fill with colour. It seemed Mr. Bennet had been right about Elizabeth being lured back home.

"Is it true that your father had taken ill?"

He couldn't stop himself from probing further to unveil the truth. He sought to be certain of the truth before he made any drastic decisions.

Jane looked away. "I am glad to say he is well, as you probably figured when you saw him earlier. The letter... it was all a misunderstanding."

"I am glad to hear that." Mr. Darcy forced a smile. "I was told you are currently preparing for Elizabeth's wedding."

Jane was silent for a moment. "Is that what my mother said?" She brought a daisy to her nose and sniffed.

"Yes," Mr. Darcy said cautiously. "She has told me that Miss Elizabeth is engaged to be married to a prince."

Jane gave a low chuckle. "It is true that Elizabeth is spending much of her time with Prince Gabriel, but he has not proposed, not yet at least. But I do believe it is only a matter of time before he does."

Mr. Darcy felt his shoulders sink with relief. Mrs. Bennet must have lied to him to keep him away. If Mr. Bennet had stayed long enough in the drawing room, he would likely have confirmed that Elizabeth was not engaged. But Mr. Darcy had learned his lesson and would not speak ill of Mrs. Bennet or anyone else in the Bennet family.

"I see," he said simply. "Is Elizabeth enjoying her time with the prince? Is she happy?" If anyone knew the truth about Elizabeth's true feelings, it would be Jane.

Jane met his gaze. "Mr. Darcy, I am not at liberty to say. Only Elizabeth can answer that question. But I *do* hope she is happy."

"Of course, Miss Bennet. Her happiness is what matters," Mr. Darcy answered. "I find myself needing to return to Netherfield. It was a pleasure speaking with you, Miss Bennet."

Jane's lips parted as though she wished to say more, but then she simply sighed and nodded.

Mr. Darcy started to walk back to his horse when he halted and turned back to Jane. "Oh, Miss Bennet," he called.

"Was there something more, Mr. Darcy?" she asked.

"I believe we have a mutual acquaintance who would call upon you, if he knew his presence would be welcome?" Mr. Darcy believed she knew it was Mr. Bingley he spoke of. By the light in her eyes and the small upturning of her lips, she knew.

"That," Jane said, "would be most acceptable."

"Very well then. I shall pass on your invitation." Mr. Darcy gave her a final nod and walked away.

On his journey back to Netherfield, he was both relieved to learn that Elizabeth was still not engaged, but also unsettled that it could happen any day.

Later in the day, over lunch, he shared his thoughts with Mr. Bingley, telling him everything he had heard about the reason why Elizabeth had to return to Longbourn with such haste.

"You mean to say Mrs. Bennet wrote a letter that claimed Mr. Bennet was ill to get her to return?"

"That is what I learned. Mrs. Bennet seemed overly excited that Elizabeth is being courted by a prince." Mr. Darcy sighed with exasperation. "In fact, she informed me of their engagement."

"They are engaged? Is it too late for you, then?"

"Well, according to Mrs. Bennet, Elizabeth and the prince are engaged, but I later found out that it was not the case."

"That is good news. It would have been so much more complicated if she had been promised to someone else. But, what if she is really happy with him? What if she is anxious for him to propose?"

"I will only know the answer to those questions when I speak to her. And I will."

"I really hope you're not setting yourself up for disappointment. Would she really want to give up a future with a prince?"

"I cannot say." Mr. Darcy scratched his temple. "But the few conversations I have had with her led me to believe that she is a romantic at heart. When she heard I was involved in separating you and Jane, she was quite disappointed."

"And that makes you believe she would marry for love?"

"I like to think so." Mr. Darcy took a swig of his rum. "And it won't be as if she'd be marrying a pauper if she chose me. But to be sure of where she stands, I have to come up with a plan to talk to her. And it will be soon."

Mr. Bingley offered his friend a few more words of encouragement, then the conversation turned to him and Jane. Mr. Darcy revealed to him that he had spoken to Jane and she was the one who had told him that Elizabeth was not yet engaged as Mrs. Bennet had claimed.

He also told him that Jane had welcomed the idea of Mr. Bingley calling on her. At hearing the news, Mr. Bingley's face brightened. It warmed Mr. Darcy's heart to witness the obvious love his friend still felt for Jane. He prayed they would have another chance.

By the time lunch came to an end, Mr. Darcy had come up with the perfect plan.

As soon as he left the table, and much to Mr. Bingley's confusion, he called for his horse once more, but this time he visited the Lucases, who had been introduced to him during his last visit. He had a favour to ask of Lady Lucas.

CHAPTER 8

Before returning to the Longbourn house,
Mr. Darcy had arranged for Mrs. Bennet to
be out of the house. He had spoken with
Lady Lucas yesterday, and talked her into
inviting Mrs. Bennet over for tea. Unable
to pass up the opportunity to discuss
Elizabeth's relationship with the prince,
Mrs. Bennet had of course accepted.

As Mr. Darcy's carriage stopped in front
of the Longbourn house, his intention was
to speak with Mr. Bennet without the
interference of Mrs. Bennet. Of course, it
would be best to speak to Elizabeth, but
Lady Lucas had mentioned to him that
each morning Elizabeth had tea with the
prince at the inn where he was staying, and
this time Jane was accompanying her.

Mr. Bennet received Mr. Darcy with a

confused expression. "I did not expect to see you back so soon after you called on us yesterday," he said, but he was smiling.

"I happened to be in the area and decided to stop by once more."

"Well, we are happy to have you. Please come inside." Mr. Bennet stepped aside to let Mr. Darcy enter.

Mr. Darcy allowed himself to be led to the drawing room, where he handed Mr. Bennet a bottle of the finest port wine. "I apologize for coming empty-handed when I visited the last time."

"You are a fine young man." Mr. Bennet held the bottle in front of him, an appreciative look on his face.

Mr. Darcy had never been called a fine man before and he found he quite liked it.

"Should we share a glass together?" Mr. Bennet asked, holding on to the bottle as though for dear life.

"I would like that very much," Mr. Darcy said.

Within a short time, the bottle was opened, the drinks were poured, and a conversation was started, about the weather and politics, and nothing personal yet. Mr. Darcy watched as Mr. Bennet enjoyed his port wine. After a few sips of his own to gather up the courage, he decided to bring up the topic that interested him the most.

"Is it true that Elizabeth did not know the prince was in Longbourn when she returned from Kent?"

Mr. Bennet took another swig of his drink and leaned back, his eyes closed. "It definitely is true." He sighed. "Prince Gabriel showed up here wanting to speak to her and when he found out she was not in residence, he had meant to leave Longbourn."

"But he changed his mind?"

"He did. With the help of my wife, who can be quite persuasive at times. She asked him to stay a little longer because she was sure Elizabeth would not be away for long."

Mr. Darcy leaned forward, his hands rested on his knees. "Mr. Bennet, it is not my place, but do you believe she is happy with the prince?"

"Who do you mean?" Mr. Bennet asked, opening his eyes. He must have had a busy morning as he had already seemed tired when he welcomed Mr. Darcy into the home.

"Elizabeth... Is she happy with the prince?" Mr. Darcy repeated his question.

Mr. Bennet was silent for a moment and then his eyes seemed to clear as he focused on Mr. Darcy's face. "Do you want to know the truth, Mr. Darcy?"

"I would appreciate it."

"I can tell you for certain that Mrs. Bennet is happier about this arrangement than Lizzy is. Of all my girls, Lizzy's character is the one I know the best."

"You believe she is not happy about a possible future with the prince?" Mr. Darcy felt hopeful.

Mr. Bennet shrugged. "I am sure she is satisfied with it, but happy, I do not believe so. In my opinion, Mrs. Bennet is much more excited."

Mr. Darcy's heart lightened as he pondered Mr. Bennet's words. "Why do you think she is not? Is it not a dream of many ladies to become a princess?"

"I always believed my Lizzy would marry for love and not simply because she desires status. She has a mind of her own, that girl." Mr. Bennet scratched his beard. "Maybe she would have been much more excited if someone else did not occupy her mind."

"May I ask who this person is?" Mr. Darcy leaned back and forced himself not to come to any conclusions.

Mr. Bennet put down his glass and folded his hands over his stomach. "Lizzy made me promise not to tell anyone this, but since her happiness is at stake, maybe you ought to know."

Mr. Darcy's eyebrows shot up in surprise. "I ought to know? What are you saying, Mr. Bennet?"

"What I am telling you, Mr. Darcy, is that my daughter returned from Kent and told me she could not stop thinking about you. Even though she made it clear her thoughts were not of a romantic nature, I could see the truth which she refused to believe. I have a feeling she would prefer you to the prince, but she doesn't want to admit it to herself."

"Me?" Mr. Darcy could not believe what he was hearing, especially since when he last spoke to Elizabeth, she did not seem to like him very much.

"That's right." Mr. Bennet picked up his glass again and refilled it, then he took a swig before leaning back his head. Seconds later, he started to snore.

Mr. Darcy remained in his chair for a long time, allowing the words to sink into his mind, to give him hope, while he listened to the sound of Mr. Bennet snoring, the glass of wine still in his hand.

He decided to remove the glass from Mr. Bennet's hand before it dropped to the floor, but when he tried, Mr. Bennet's fingers tightened around it. His eyes glazed over, he shook his head and took another swig even though he'd had a few too many already.

It was not long after he fell asleep again that Mr. Darcy felt it was best for him to leave. After all, he had the information he needed. "Mr. Bennet, I should get going." He tapped the older man on the shoulder.

At that moment, Mr. Bennet perked up again. All of a sudden, he looked as though he had not been sleeping at all, even though his eyes were still clouded.

"Mr. Darcy," he said. "I do not know you very well, but if being with you would make my daughter happy, I would be content as well."

Mr. Darcy leaned forward. "So you do not mind if she does not end up marrying the prince?"

"Let's just say, I am not as fascinated about the prince as Mrs. Bennet is. Elizabeth's happiness is my priority."

"What is it you think I should do, Mr. Bennet? You know your daughter better than anyone."

"Indeed, I do." A smile made his face glow with pride. "What exactly would you like me to help you with?"

"Do you not believe it is too late for Elizabeth and me?"

"Before I answer that question, I have a question for you, Mr. Darcy. What is it you feel for my Elizabeth? Is the feeling mutual?"

"Unfortunately, I am not able to answer that question at the present. I can only say that my feelings are true and honorable." Anything else Mr. Darcy planned to say concerning his feelings for Elizabeth, would be communicated to her first.

"Is that a no, then?" Mr. Bennet asked, eyes narrowed.

"How I feel for Elizabeth at this point is not important until I know for sure that she is not fully happy with the prince. If that turns out to be the case, I shall gladly revisit the topic."

"Do you intend on speaking to her?" Mr. Bennet asked.

"Perhaps." He had to find out the truth from Elizabeth. Should he discover that Mr. Bennet's suspicions are correct, he would not hesitate to convince her of the sincerity of his emotions.

On the other hand, Elizabeth is a woman of integrity and she might be hesitant to break the prince's heart. If she chooses to stay with the prince, Mr. Darcy would, of course, step aside and allow her to find happiness with another man.

"Whatever you decide to do, I wish you the best of luck." Mr. Bennet showed Mr. Darcy to the door and the two men parted on pleasant terms.

Back at Netherfield, Mr. Bingley was waiting impatiently to hear how Mr.

Darcy's visit to the Longbourn house had gone. But also to find out if he had seen Jane again. Unfortunately this time, Jane and Elizabeth had not returned from the inn before Mr. Darcy left. Mr. Bingley was disappointed to hear that. He had yet to gain the courage to call upon the eldest Bennet daughter.

"My dear friend," Mr. Darcy said, "Whether I saw Jane or not, would not help you in any way. I suggest you go and speak to her."

"But I have been silent for far too long. I walked out of her life with no explanation. What if she no longer wants anything to do with me?"

"You will not know the answer to that question unless you leave Netherfield Park and find that out for yourself. Just as I intend to find out the truth of Elizabeth's feelings directly from her."

"What if things do not work out the way you wish they would? What if she chooses the prince?"

"Then at least I would have tried. Not knowing is more painful than facing the truth, however bitter it may be."

"That's very brave," Mr. Bingley said. "But you are aware that if Elizabeth chooses you, you would have Mrs. Bennet's wrath to contend with, right?"

Mr. Darcy chuckled. Even Mrs. Bennet's wrath was not strong enough to scare him off. "If Elizabeth chooses me, whatever obstacles I have to face would all be worth it. Who knows, perhaps once I get to know Mrs. Bennet a little better, I might find I quite like her."

"True." Mr. Bingley shook his head in admiration. "It is rather commendable to see you go after what you want."

"I wish you would do the same," Mr. Darcy said.

"Maybe I will." Mr. Bingley rubbed his forehead. "Maybe I will."

"Wonderful." Mr. Darcy rose from his seat. "I should get going. I have important things to take care of in Meryton. Would you care to accompany me?"

"Actually, why not? Perhaps getting out there would give me the courage to visit Jane."

"That's what I like to hear." Mr. Darcy clapped his friend on the back and together they walked out of the house. It was time for Mr. Darcy to put his plan in motion.

CHAPTER 9

Mrs. Bennet and her eldest girls stood in front of the house, awaiting Kitty's arrival. Mr. Bennet had decided to remain in the parlour as the wait had been too long for him.

Kitty had been away visiting Lydia in Cambridge, as Lydia needed someone to be by her side during the early days of her pregnancy.

As soon as the news of the pregnancy had arrived, Mr. Bennet had urged Mrs. Bennet to accompany Kitty to Cambridge and overjoyed at becoming a grandmother, Mrs. Bennet had quickly packed. But as soon as the prince showed up on the doorstep, she changed her mind, saying she would visit Lydia as soon as the prince proposed to Elizabeth, which she had been certain would happen.

She had wanted to ensure that Elizabeth did not reject him the way she had turned down Mr. Collins. Her daughter was strong-willed, and if her heart was not with the prince, she would not hesitate to refuse his proposal.

The carriage finally arrived, and Kitty poked her head out of the window, her face all smiles. But when she got out of the carriage, they were all surprised to see that Lydia was with her.

Elizabeth glanced at her mother, unable to believe that her pregnant sister would not stay behind in Cambridge to rest. But it was a lovely surprise and an honor to be able to witness Lydia's pregnancy with her own eyes. She only hoped the journey was not too tiresome for her.

Elizabeth hugged both of her sisters as she had missed them so much. Excitement filled the air as more embraces were shared and the sisters shared the joy brought on by the idea of a new baby being part of the family in less than six months.

When Lydia went to embrace her mother, the embrace though affectionate, only lasted a moment before Mrs. Bennet pulled away and placed a hand on Lydia's stomach. "Lydia, you silly girl. You are with child. What brings you here when you should be resting?"

Lydia dismissed her mother's concerns with a mischievous grin. "Mother, do not be like Mr. Wickham. He has been treating me like an invalid. I am with child, not ill." She searched Elizabeth's face. "Now, where is the handsome prince?"

"Is that why you came?" Elizabeth asked, laughter pouring out of her.

"Of course." Lydia rubbed her hands together. "I needed to come and see him with my own eyes. I wanted to witness the proposal. It hasn't happened yet, has it?"

Elizabeth shook her head and lowered her gaze. The prince had not yet proposed, even if they had been spending quite a lot of time together. What if he never proposed? That would mean Lydia had come all this way for nothing.

"The prince is not here." Elizabeth went to Lydia and placed an arm around her shoulders. "He is staying at the Rosewood Inn in Meryton. But he will be joining us for supper."

Lydia's shoulders sank, but only for a moment before her eyes shone with renewed excitement. "Is he a real prince?"

"Of course he is," Mrs. Bennet answered quickly.

"And where is Papa?" Kitty and Lydia both asked at the same time. They did not wait for the response as they hurried into the house to find him. They knew he would be in the parlour or the library, possibly fast asleep. He could never sit in a chair for a length of time without nodding off.

They all found Mr. Bennet inside the parlour and he was happy to see both of them, and just as surprised to see that Lydia had come as well. They all gathered inside the room to talk about the baby and took turns at touching Lydia's slightly swollen stomach. Once they had all settled down, out of nowhere Lydia mentioned that Mr. Darcy and Mr. Bingley were in town on business.

"We saw them when the carriage drove through Meryton."

Upon hearing Mr. Darcy's name,

Elizabeth's heart began to race. Her father had mentioned to her that Mr. Darcy had called upon him several days ago but had not said what the reason for the visit was. When Elizabeth had pressed him, Mrs. Bennet had changed the subject back to the prince, as usual. But she *did* add that she had found Mr. Darcy to be quite arrogant.

Later that night, Jane admitted to Elizabeth that during his visit Mr. Darcy had inquired about her. In spite of herself, Elizabeth had felt a warmth spreading through her chest, but she had ignored the sensation. She told herself it meant nothing and avoided any topic of Mr. Darcy until now.

Now that Lydia had brought up Mr. Darcy again, Elizabeth was unable to stop wondering exactly why he had returned to Hertfordshire.

Next to her, she could see that the colour had left Jane's face. She had to be wondering the same thing about Mr. Bingley. She had told Elizabeth that she had made it known to Mr. Darcy that he was welcome to call on her, but he had still not called on her.

In spite of Mr. Darcy asking Jane about her, Elizabeth had no reason to believe he had called at Longbourn for her benefit. He couldn't have as when they had parted ways in Kent, it had been on unpleasant terms and she had thought they would not see each other again any time soon.

During lunch, Kitty brought up the subject again and went on to say that they had a quick but polite conversation with the two gentlemen.

"I have to say that Mr. Darcy surprised me," Kitty said. "He was not as despicable as many think him to be."

"I agree," Lydia said. "Do not be fooled by the hard exterior. Inside his heart, Mr. Darcy is a good and generous man."

"What makes you say that?" Elizabeth asked before she could think about it. Then she lowered her gaze back to her meal, continuing to eat as though the question was one anybody would be interested in knowing an answer to.

Lydia leaned forward, her eyes sparkling. "I was told not to reveal this information, but Mr. Darcy was the one who paid for my wedding to Mr. Wickham and also settled his debts."

"Goodness." Mrs. Bennet brought a hand to her cheek. "Why in the world have you not mentioned this before?"

"Because Mr. Darcy did not wish for anyone to know. He had sworn Mr. Wickham and me to secrecy." She shrugged. "He said it was a private wedding gift to us and no one needed to know. Can you believe he did all that for us?"

"I cannot," Mrs. Bennet said while Mr. Bennet ate his meal in silence. He did not seem at all surprised that Mr. Darcy would do such a thing. Did he already know?

Elizabeth would never have thought of Mr. Darcy to be quite so generous, and to do such a good deed without making sure everyone knew about it in order to receive their praise.

Lydia and Mr. Wickham had met at the Meryton Ball, but soon after, they ran off together. For days, scandal had surrounded the Bennet family until news arrived that they were to be married. Elizabeth would never have imagined that Mr. Darcy would be the one to remove the stain from their family's name.

As she tried to digest both her food and the new information, she felt Jane's eyes on her and for no known reason, she felt herself blushing.

"So, Mr. Darcy fooled all of us? Is that what you're saying?" Jane asked, still staring at Elizabeth.

Lydia nodded. "If by that you mean he led us all to believe he was rather cold and unapproachable when in fact he has one of the kindest hearts I have ever known, then yes. He had indeed fooled all of us."

Still unable to believe the news, Elizabeth said no more as Lydia continued to praise Mr. Darcy as though he was a hero. She found it hard to see Mr. Darcy in another light, after spending such energy in despising him. And now everyone, including Mrs. Bennet, was praising him.

"I always suspected that maybe he wasn't as bad as everyone made him out to be," their mother said, gazing into space.

Elizabeth found her reaction amusing as the words Mrs. Bennet had used to describe Mr. Darcy before she heard

Lydia's news had been far from pleasant. Elizabeth had not blamed her for taking a dislike to the man as she had also felt the same about him. But Mrs. Bennet loathed to be wrong about anything or anyone.

Unable to handle the conflicted emotions the conversation about Mr. Darcy brought up, Elizabeth changed the subject back to Lydia's pregnancy, which had not yet received as much attention as it should have.

Lydia was all too happy to talk about her unborn child, and after the meal, the family moved to the library, where Mr. Bennet sank into his chair and read while the sisters and Mrs. Bennet continued talking about the baby. Even if it was early days yet and it would be a while before Lydia's stomach grew and the baby started to move, Mrs. Bennet was already discussing the possible names for the child.

The day went by rather fast with the sisters enjoying their time together and Prince Gabriel arrived for supper with chocolates for Elizabeth. But before he could hand the chocolates to her, Mrs. Bennet reached for them.

"Thank you, my dear Prince." Mrs. Bennet beamed. "I will enjoy these."

Elizabeth found herself laughing. She was used to her mother making everything about her. Upon hearing that the chocolates had come from France, Mrs. Bennet opened the box immediately and popped a round chocolate into her mouth. She closed her eyes to better relish the taste, her cheeks glowing.

It took a moment for her to realize that she had been so excited by the chocolate that she had not invited the prince into the house.

"Silly me," she said, still chewing the chocolate. "Prince Gabriel, please come in. Dinner approaches quickly."

Dinner was pleasant and Lydia and Kitty bombarded the prince with questions, which came faster than he could answer them. Even though Lydia was pregnant and married, she flirted slightly with the prince. The air was so lively that no one seemed to mind and simply laughed her behavior off.

"Prince Gabriel," Kitty said when dessert was served, "when do you intend on returning to France?"

"Very soon, I expect." He glanced at Elizabeth. "My parents are expecting me in a week or so."

"We cannot wait to meet your parents in person," Mrs. Bennet added, and Elizabeth felt embarrassed as he had not even proposed yet. "To raise such a wonderful young man, they have to be wonderful themselves."

"And they are." Under Prince Gabriel's gaze, Elizabeth felt her cheeks warming up. She looked away.

She prayed that her mother would not pressure the prince too much into proposing. She wanted the decision to come from him, not because her mother pushed hard enough. She could be so overwhelming sometimes. No wonder the Bennet family had left such a bad taste in Mr. Darcy's mouth.

"France must be a beautiful country," Kitty said, wanting to hear more about the country they had never seen before.

The prince was all too happy to launch into another description of his country.

Elizabeth was finding that she was no

longer as excited at the prospect of seeing France, and during the conversation, her mind kept drifting away. She was almost relieved when the meal came to an end and Prince Gabriel took his leave.

"It was a pleasure to see you again, Elizabeth, and to meet your two other sisters," he said when Elizabeth walked him to the carriage. "They are quite lively. I do hope you and I will get to see each other again before I leave for France."

"I do not see any reason why not," Elizabeth said.

"We should return to the gallery again in Meryton before I leave. I thoroughly enjoyed our time there."

"Yes," Elizabeth said. "Certainly. When exactly do you plan to leave?"

"I wish to be back in France before the week has begun again."

"I see." Elizabeth felt uneasy somehow.

Prince Gabriel got into his carriage and waved at Elizabeth from the window. She waved back as the carriage pulled away. Would he leave England without proposing? She found it strange that he would spend so much time with her and not ask for her hand. Perhaps he was having second thoughts. But if he was, why would he still want to see her?

When Jane and Elizabeth were getting ready for bed, she voiced her concerns about going to Meryton with Prince Gabriel in case she came across Mr. Darcy.

"I am curious," Jane said. "Has what Lydia said about Mr. Darcy changed him in your eyes?"

"Not quite." Elizabeth averted her gaze. "We do not know for sure that what Lydia said was true."

"I see no reason why she would make something like that up."

"You have a point." Elizabeth did not tell her sister that despite all the good things Mr. Darcy apparently did, he still did some rather unforgivable things, such as keeping her and Mr. Bingley apart. It was hard for her to merge the two Mr. Darcys together in her mind. "I would still prefer not to see him again."

"And I still believe you feel something for him, but you're trying to run from your feelings."

Elizabeth met her sister's eyes again.

"Trust me, Jane, that is not the case."

Jane shrugged. "All right then." She still seemed unconvinced, but she changed the subject. "Do you believe Prince Gabriel will ask you to marry him before he returns to France?"

Elizabeth sighed. "I am honestly not sure."

"If he does, would you agree to become his wife?"

Elizabeth mulled the question over in silence. "I think it is best we wait and see if he proposes at all. There's still a chance he might not."

As much as Elizabeth enjoyed her time with the prince, she was still conflicted about what her response to his proposal would be.

CHAPTER 10

Elizabeth was shocked that Mr. Darcy still resided in her thoughts when she awoke the next morning. He had been the last person on her mind when she had fallen asleep.

She was still in her own world as she showed up for breakfast with her family. Although she was present at the table, her mind was far away, back in Kent. She kept asking herself what Mr. Darcy had wanted to say to her. He had mentioned that it was important, but she had ignored him, believing it the right thing to do at the time. But was it? If she had listened, if she had been more courteous, she wouldn't be asking herself these questions right now.

"Are you troubled, Elizabeth?" Mrs. Bennet asked after she had been talking about Prince Gabriel for a time with no reaction from Elizabeth. "You seem awfully quiet this morning. Are you unwell?"

"No, mother. I am perfectly all right. I simply have a lot on my mind today."

"I should hope you're thinking about the prince." Mrs. Bennet raised an eyebrow. "He is such a handsome man and so kind and generous. Those chocolates he gave me were delicious. They tasted quite expensive."

"You mean the chocolates he brought for Elizabeth?" Kitty laughed. "As I recall, he was about to give them to her."

Mrs. Bennet threw her a disapproving look. "Kitty, watch your mouth."

Everyone at the table laughed, but the sounds of laughter were broken by that of a carriage approaching the grounds. Mrs. Bennet jumped up from the table and rushed to the dining room window to see who had come to visit them. A squeal of delight burst from her lips as she spun around, her hands on her cheeks. "He's returned."

Before anyone could ask who she

meant, she hurried out of the room. Elizabeth and her sisters went to the window to see for themselves while Mr. Bennet remained in his seat, reading his paper.

As Elizabeth had suspected, it was Prince Gabriel. But he had not mentioned that he would return today. Or so early.

"He is back so soon?" Lydia breathed with excitement.

They all turned to the door when Mrs. Bennet returned not long after she left, smoothing down her dress. While they watched, she lowered herself back into her chair and turned to Mr. Bennet.

"Mr. Bennet, you should go and welcome the prince into the house. We do not want to seem too eager." She glanced around the table. "I am certain the prince has returned so soon because he is finally ready to propose to Elizabeth."

Mr. Bennet gave her an amused look and stood up from his chair and left the room.

"Lizzy," Mrs. Bennet said. "You should go and make yourself presentable." She suddenly shot out of her chair again, forgetting her composure and began to fuss with Elizabeth's hair, tucking flyaway strands behind her ears. "And you should try not to look too desperate."

"I do not have to try, Mama. I am not desperate."

"Shush," she said, glancing at the door. "Do not let the prince hear you say that. Of course you're desperate, just do not show it."

It took some time for Mr. Bennet and Prince Gabriel to come to the dining room, and when they did, their expressions were serious. Elizabeth guessed that they had made a stop in the parlour to have a discussion.

Her hands started to sweat when she suspected that her mother was right. The prince had likely asked Mr. Bennet for his blessing.

She held her breath as she stood to greet him while her sisters watched in anticipation.

"Prince Gabriel." She managed a smile. "I did not expect you to return so soon."

"Neither did I." He glanced at everyone around the table. "May I have a moment with Elizabeth?"

"Of course. Everyone come, we must let them have their privacy." Mrs. Bennet couldn't stand up fast enough. Within seconds, she had gathered her daughters and husband and ushered them out of the room.

Elizabeth sat back down and clasped her hands tight in her lap as the prince pulled out a chair for himself. "Is everything all right, Prince Gabriel?"

"Of course." A smile played on his lips. "I am always in good spirits whenever I see you, Elizabeth."

"That is very kind of you to say." Elizabeth could feel the sweat appearing on her upper lip but she refrained from wiping it away for fear he would notice she was nervous.

"Elizabeth, I have thoroughly enjoyed the last days we spent in each other's company." He gazed deep into her eyes. "As you know, I will be returning to France in only a few days. And I have to admit I am finding it hard to part with you."

"I have enjoyed our time together as

well, Prince Gabriel." Elizabeth felt it was the right and polite thing for her to say.

"I am glad to hear that. But we have not had a chance to thoroughly discuss how we will move forward."

Elizabeth glanced at the door when she heard a shuffling sound. She knew very well that her mother and sisters had gathered on the other side of the door, listening to the entire conversation. She felt her cheeks flush with embarrassment but gathered her composure as she focused on the prince. "No, we have not." She was still unsure of whether she was ready for this conversation, but he was too kind of a man for her to dismiss him without hearing him out.

Prince Gabriel pushed his chair back and rested his hands on his knees. "I am sure you're aware that I am quite fond of you. I appreciate how you think and carry yourself. You are a beautiful and intelligent woman."

"Intelligent?" Elizabeth raised an eyebrow. But she was flattered by his words.

"Intelligence comes in many forms, Miss

Bennet, and I believe you're one of those people who are quietly intelligent."

"You're very kind, Prince Gabriel."

"I am simply being honest." He swept a hand across his forehead. "I am quite excited about a future with you."

Elizabeth leaned back in her chair and waited for him to continue, even though she knew where the conversation was headed. She was not sure if she was elated or terrified.

"But I must admit that there is something which concerns me, no matter how I try to dissuade myself," he said.

Elizabeth frowned. "What's that?"

"When we spent time together, a part of me couldn't help but feel that you were not fully present in the moment." He shifted his chair forward. "Before we discuss the future, I would like to know if there is something about me that makes you uncomfortable in some way."

"No, Prince Gabriel, of course not." Elizabeth felt ashamed of herself for making him feel that way even if it had not been her intention. "I am very sorry if I gave you that impression. You are a very kind man and I truly enjoyed spending time with you as well."

"If that is the case, why are you not able to be fully present when you are with me?"

Elizabeth hung her head. "You are correct in thinking that I was sometimes distracted during our excursions. Often I found my thoughts lost in a matter from the past that I have yet to resolve. For that I apologize."

"I accept your apology and hope that during the time we spend together after today, I will be all you think about."

Elizabeth hesitated, but nodded. She folded her hands tighter in her lap as the prince rose from his chair and came to her.

Her heart fluttered when he dropped on one knee and gazed into her eyes. "Miss Elizabeth Bennet, now that there's nothing more standing in the way of us moving forward, I have something important to ask you."

"Prince Gabriel," Elizabeth said suddenly as though she wanted to stop him.

"Is something wrong?" He tilted his head to the side.

"No," Elizabeth whispered. "Please, go on." The moment reminded her of the day Mr. Collins had proposed to her and she had been uncomfortable. But this was different. Prince Gabriel could never compare to Mr. Collins. She forced herself to think only of the gentleman in front of her, and none other.

"What I was about to say is that I feel quite drawn to you. I do not regret the decision to come back to England to see you. The only regret I would have would be to return to France without asking you to spend your future with me as my wife." With that, the prince took Elizabeth's hands in his. She cringed when she felt the sweat coating them. It seemed he was as nervous as she was. She found it endearing that he wasn't overly confident.

"Miss Elizabeth Bennet, would you agree to be my wife? I would love nothing more than to make you my princess. It would be a dream to see our worlds merging into one."

Elizabeth's head told her to say yes immediately, but she found her heart was conflicted yet again. What reason was there for her to reject his proposal? He was a kind and intelligent men and he cared for her. He was the kind of man she could see a future with. And in addition to that, he was one of the most attractive men she had ever seen. What made him even more attractive was the fact that he never flaunted his good looks or his wealth. His humbleness drew her to him in a way that another's pride drove her away.

Elizabeth mulled his words over. She could not find a logical reason why she should turn him down. He was kind and attentive to her and accepted her family.

She allowed a smile to warm her face and before her heart could talk her out of it, she gave him his answer. "Prince Gabriel, I would love nothing more than to be your wife."

She had made a choice and, right then, she felt it was the right one.

Prince Gabriel clearly felt the same as he lifted himself from the floor and pulled Elizabeth to her feet, still holding her hands. "You have just made me the happiest of men." He lifted one of her hands to his lips and kissed it. "I will make you the happiest princess there ever was. And I cannot wait to show you my country of France."

"I also cannot wait to see it with you by my side." Elizabeth refrained from analyzing her decision and instead made sure she was in the moment.

Suddenly the door opened and Mrs. Bennet and her sisters entered to congratulate them.

"We are so very happy for you." Jane hugged Elizabeth tight, followed by her mother, then Lydia and Kitty.

Mr. Bennet remained in the doorway with a smile on his face which seemed forced. But finally, he stepped into the room and pulled Elizabeth into his arms as well "I hope you're happy," he said into her ear.

"I am, Papa." She squeezed him tighter. That was all he ever wanted for her, true happiness.

Elizabeth did not know what tomorrow would bring, but at this moment what she felt resembled happiness.

Already the discussions of the wedding plans started. Not long after, Mrs. Bennet asked Mr. Bennet to accompany her to the Lucases.

Elizabeth was sure her mother would share the good news with everyone they met along the way. She had been convinced from the start the prince would propose and now that he had, she couldn't be happier.

Not long after Mr. and Mrs. Bennet left, Prince Gabriel did as well, with the promise of returning in the morning to join them for a celebratory breakfast.

The moment he walked through the door and Elizabeth was alone with her thoughts, she wrapped a hand around her throat, suddenly unable to breathe. Jane noticed her distress immediately and pulled her aside.

"What's going on, Elizabeth? You look pale."

"Jane," Elizabeth said, trembling. "What if... What if I made the wrong choice?"

Jane's eyes widened in horror. "Oh, Elizabeth. You cannot think like that."

"I cannot help it." Elizabeth buried her head in her hands. The only person who can answer the question she just asked Jane was herself. What frightened her was that she probably knew the answer and did not want to admit it to herself.

CHAPTER 11

Elizabeth and Jane no longer discussed Elizabeth's conflicted feelings until later in the day when they were alone in the room. Mr. and Mrs. Bennet were still at the Lucases, and Kitty was keeping Lydia company while she rested.

"I do not understand, Lizzy," Jane said. "You seemed excited when Prince Gabriel proposed."

Elizabeth sighed and sat on the bed. "In the moment, I was. It felt right at the time. Now, I am not so sure." She felt terrible for agreeing to the proposal when there was a moment before the prince asked her to marry him when she had felt uneasy.

"So you feel you made the wrong choice?" Jane looked as confused as Elizabeth felt.

"I do not know." Elizabeth buried her head in her hands. "The truth is, Jane, there's someone I cannot stop thinking about."

"Mr. Darcy," Jane sank down onto the bed next to Elizabeth. "Am I right?"

Elizabeth nodded. "I do not know why, but I still cannot help but think of him nearly every free moment."

Jane took Elizabeth's hand. "Oh, Lizzy. What's happening here?"

"I wish I knew. I really do." Elizabeth wrapped her arms around her body. "I do not know what's become of me."

"As your sister who loves you deeply, my advice is that you should tell the prince the truth."

Elizabeth's body tensed. "What truth exactly? That I have been thinking of Mr. Darcy? I cannot—"

"No, not that. But he should know that you do not feel the same way."

"But he was so overjoyed when I agreed to marry him, Jane. I could not stand to break his heart."

"I understand that," Jane said. "But I think if you're having doubts, it is best you tell him now before the wedding preparations begin. Before it becomes too late and you risk scandal."

Elizabeth felt an ache deep in her heart. What Jane was saying made sense. "He would be so disappointed. So would Mama."

"Of course Mama will be disappointed, but she will have no choice but to accept it...in time." Jane turned to face Elizabeth. "You know yourself, Lizzy. You are a true romantic and I cannot see you marrying someone you do not love."

"But I am also someone who keeps her word. I made Prince Gabriel a promise. How could I go back on it?"

"I know, and I understand how hard this must be for you." Jane touched a lock of Elizabeth's hair. "Do you have any feelings for Prince Gabriel at all?"

"I believe him to be a good man. He is kind, intelligent, and respectful towards women. I know he will be good to me." Elizabeth chewed on her bottom lip. "And I do care for him. At the same time, there's something stopping me from feeling completely for him."

"And you are prepared to enter into a marriage feeling like that?"

"I do not know. One thing I do know for sure is that I made a promise. It is not as if women must always be enthralled with their affianced." Elizabeth shrugged. "Perhaps if I give him a real chance, I will stop feeling this way. Sooner or later I will stop thinking about Mr. Darcy. Maybe I am just thinking of him a lot more because of what Lydia said." Elizabeth shook her head. "No, Jane. I cannot allow Mr. Darcy to stand in the way of what could be a good marriage. Prince Gabriel will make a very fine husband."

"It does not matter what I say, my dear Elizabeth. You should do what you think is right for you."

"You're right." Elizabeth straightened up. "And the right thing to do would be to keep my promise to Prince Gabriel."

Their conversation was disturbed by Mr. and Mrs. Bennet's return home. Their mother came into the room to tell them to go to the drawing room immediately as they had wedding plans to discuss.

Feeling more comfortable with her

decision, Elizabeth went along with everything, even though Jane looked at her with a worried expression from time to time. Although the wedding date had not even been set yet, Mrs. Bennet was already discussing flowers, decorations, and the wedding cake. Elizabeth did not have the energy to tell her not to get carried away.

"We will be hosting a royal wedding," Mrs. Bennet said. "Everything has to be perfect." She looked at Mr. Bennet, who looked increasingly uneasy as Mrs. Bennet listed all the things which she insisted had to be part of the wedding. From the sound of things, it would cost a fortune.

"Slow down, my dear," he finally said. "This is Lizzy's wedding. Shouldn't we be asking what her preferences are?"

"That's ridiculous." Mrs. Bennet threw her arms in the air. "Lizzy has never been married. What would she know about planning a wedding?"

Elizabeth gave Mr. Bennet a secret smile. "It is okay, Papa. It will be Mama's day as much as mine. It will be a special day for all of us."

When the excitement eventually settled

and everyone became occupied with other matters, Mr. Bennet asked Elizabeth to accompany him on a short walk. Elizabeth, who had always enjoyed her walks with him, agreed immediately.

Outside, the evening air was comfortably cool and birds chirped in the trees. They walked for quite a distance before Mr. Bennet stopped and turned to his daughter. "I would like you to be honest with me, Elizabeth."

She nodded. "Of course, Papa."

"Are you happy? Are you completely happy?"

Fortunately, Elizabeth had had enough time to pull herself together and to clear her mind of Mr. Darcy. She was ready to focus on her relationship with Prince Gabriel. "I think I am, Papa. I truly think I am happy."

"That's not good enough, my dear girl." Mr. Bennet took her hand and they started to walk again. "Thinking you're happy is not the same as knowing. So what is it? Are you happy with the prince? I do hope you're not feeling pushed into the royal wedding by your mother."

"Not at all. Agreeing to marry Prince Gabriel was entirely my decision. He will make a fine husband."

"I have no doubt that he will." Mr. Bennet's expression softened. "But you are a free spirit, Elizabeth. My wish for you has always been that you will marry a man who allows you the freedom to be yourself. I would not like you to feel stifled in any way."

"Thank you, Papa. Your words mean the world to me."

Mr. Bennet put an arm around her shoulders. "You should know that I am always here for you, no matter what you decide."

Elizabeth hesitated before she responded. "What do you mean, Papa?"

"If marrying the prince is the right decision for you, I will support that decision." He coughed. "But if at any point you decide to change your mind, I will still support you. No matter what your mother says."

"Thank you." Elizabeth wondered whether he knew that she had been having doubts even if she had never said a word to him.

"Another thing," Mr. Bennet cut through her thoughts. "Do not let your mother take over your wedding. Plan your day as you see fit."

"But she was right," Elizabeth said, laughing. "I do not have experience when it comes to weddings. I do not mind allowing her to take the lead."

"Very well. I am just happy that you're happy."

They continued their walk for a while, but when Mr. Bennet suggested they return to the house, Elizabeth told him she would stay outside for a moment.

When he left her alone, she sat down on a fallen log to enjoy the nature and think about everything that had happened that day and how it would impact the rest of her life.

She was about to become a wife, and not just any wife, but the wife of a prince. As the idea of becoming a princess started to sink in, without warning, her thoughts returned to Mr. Darcy. The man was like a thief in the night, coming to steal her thoughts. He crept into her mind every time she was alone.

Suddenly, the same questions she had asked herself earlier came back to haunt her. She hated feeling this way, especially after telling her father she was happy.

She did not understand why thoughts of Mr. Darcy unraveled her so. If she chose not to marry the prince, it did not even mean anything would happen between them. She did not even have a reason to believe Mr. Darcy felt anything but indifference towards her, which was exactly how she felt about him as well. Wasn't it?

Desperate to banish him from her mind and stand by her decision, Elizabeth stood up again and returned to the house where she found her mother still going on about the wedding. She did not even consider that Prince Gabriel's family may also want to have a say in the preparations.

After dinner, Elizabeth excused herself to go to bed earlier than the rest. As she settled down to sleep, she decided that she would try to enjoy herself. She was about to experience every woman's fairytale, and she could not stand in her own way.

One day, when she was happily married to Prince Gabriel, she would look back on this day and think how silly she had been to have considered breaking off her engagement.

Instead of worrying herself to sleep, this time Elizabeth fell asleep with a small smile on her face.

CHAPTER 12

❧

In the morning, Jane asked Elizabeth again about whether she was still thinking about Mr. Darcy and having doubts about the prince.

While they spoke, Mrs. Bennet happened to be walking past their bedroom door and overheard their conversation.

She was frantic as she ran to find her husband. "Mr. Bennet, I think Mr. Darcy has spoken to Elizabeth." Her breath came out in gasps and she was panting so hard she could barely get the words out.

"What brings you to that conclusion?" Mr. Bennet asked.

"I overheard her and Jane talking about him just now." She dropped into a chair and her face grew serious as her eyes focused on Mr. Bennet's surprised face. "Please, Mr. Bennet, you must go and see Mr. Darcy immediately. Tell him to stay away from our Elizabeth. We cannot allow anything to stand in the way of her marriage to our prince."

"Mrs. Bennet, Elizabeth is still free to talk to whomever she wants."

Mrs. Bennet let out a frustrated breath. "Of course she can talk to anyone, but not to Mr. Darcy."

"Do you not think it is unfair of you to say that after everything Mr. Darcy has done for Lydia and Mr. Wickham?"

Mrs. Bennet was quiet for a long time and when she spoke, her voice was calmer. "It was very kind of him to do what he did, but that does not mean he can stand in the way of Elizabeth's happiness with Prince Gabriel."

Mr. Bennet put away the book he was reading. "What exactly would you have me do?"

"You should go to Netherfield at once. Make sure Mr. Darcy does not speak to Elizabeth until the wedding has happened." Mrs. Bennet paced the room.

"Go in the pretense of wanting to thank him for his kindness towards Lydia and Mr. Wickham."

"I will do no such thing. As Lydia said, Mr. Darcy does not wish for us to know about his good deed."

"Very well." Mrs. Bennet placed her hands on the armrests of her chair. "I still think you should pay him a visit. Say you will at least think about it."

"I will think about it," Mr. Bennet said and returned to his book.

Mrs. Bennet continued to talk about the wedding, not minding that Mr. Bennet was barely paying her any attention.

Soon after breakfast, Mrs. Bennet urged him again to visit Netherfield. This time he relented simply from a desire that she would leave him in peace.

He left the house without telling his daughters where he was going.

As the carriage drew away from the house, Mrs. Bennet stood by the window waving frantically.

When Mr. Bennet arrived at Netherfield Park, it was Mr. Bingley who welcomed him into the house.

"Mr. Bennet, how wonderful to see you again." Mr. Bingley looked uncomfortable as he greeted the older man, and he had the right to be after the way he had treated Jane. "What brings you here?"

"I came to see Mr. Darcy. Is he around?"

"He certainly is. You will find him in the studio. The footman will take you there."

As soon as Mr. Bennet stepped into the studio, and saw the paintings around the room, it did not take him long to realize what was going on. He gazed from one painting in particular to Mr. Darcy with a knowing expression, but he refrained from saying a word.

He was unable to hide a smile as he greeted Mr. Darcy. "It is nice to see you again, Mr. Darcy. Good to see you are well."

"Thank you, Mr. Bennet." Mr. Darcy left a smear of white paint on Mr. Bennet as they shook hands. "What brings you here? I hope all is well."

"Perfectly. I just happened to be in the area and thought I would pass by to say hello. Especially since I thoroughly enjoyed our last conversation."

"So did I." Mr. Darcy put the brush away. "I had planned on visiting again, but I have been rather busy."

Mr. Bennet glanced from one painting to the next. "I can see that. I had no idea you are a painter."

"I am not." Mr. Darcy smirked. "But I find it to be quite relaxing."

"In that case," said Mr. Bennet, "I will leave you to continue. I did not intend on staying long."

Mr. Darcy told him there was no need for him to leave so soon and invited him to join him for a drink. Mr. Bennet accepted only one cup of tea and drank it while they discussed the harvest that year. Soon after, he excused himself, claiming he had work to do at the house.

* * *

As Mr. Bennet's carriage pulled away, Mr. Darcy watched from the window of the studio, a deep frown between his eyes. He had a feeling there had been another reason behind Mr. Bennet's visit.

He was just thinking about what that reason could be, when Mr. Bingley walked into the studio.

"Why did he leave so soon and in such a hurry?"

"My guess is as good as yours," Mr. Darcy said, returning to his paintings.

"Interesting," Mr. Bingley said. "Did he say why he stopped by?"

"He simply said he was in the area and wished to say hello."

"I do not know." Mr. Bingley moved to the window. "I have a feeling he came here to discuss something with you and did not have the courage to do it, in the end."

"Maybe what he came to say was not that important." Mr. Darcy wondered whether it had something to do with Elizabeth. When he last visited the Longbourn house, Mr. Bennet had been open to him pursuing Elizabeth. Now he feared that perhaps he had changed his mind and had come to tell him as much.

Mr. Bingley turned his back to the window. "What did he think of the paintings?"

Mr. Darcy looked up, his brow still wrinkled. "I find it rather strange that he hardly made a comment about them."

"You're right, that is strange. And how do *you* feel about them?" Mr. Bingley walked up to one of the paintings and studied it for a moment. "Are you pleased with how they turned out?"

"Not at all." Mr. Darcy had lied when he told Mr. Bennet that painting was relaxing. It was the most frustrating activity he had ever taken on. "Painting has never been my strength as you can see from my works of art."

Mr. Bingley rubbed his chin. "I disagree. I do not think they're so awful. And painting does seem to be taking your mind off things."

"You are a good friend, Bingley. I appreciate that."

Mr. Bingley lowered himself into an empty chair and watched in silence as Mr. Darcy worked. When he finally spoke, his voice was thick with concern. "My dear friend, there's something I have been meaning to tell you."

"Is that so?" Mr. Darcy turned toward him, wiping his hands on a rag. "It must be something serious for you to look like that."

"It has to do with Elizabeth. I was not sure whether you would want to hear it, but you will find out sooner or later."

Upon hearing Elizabeth's name, Mr. Darcy's heart started to gallop. "What is it, Bingley?"

"I happened to hear from one of the footmen last night that Elizabeth Bennet is now engaged to the prince."

The words hit Mr. Darcy so hard he stumbled towards an empty chair and dropped into it. "She has agreed to be his wife?"

"I am afraid so. Apparently, it is the talk of town at the moment and Mrs. Bennet is ecstatic, as you can imagine."

"I am certain she is." Mr. Darcy's voice came out in barely a whisper. What could he do now? He couldn't possibly go to Elizabeth and beg her to reconsider, to choose him instead. He believed her to be a woman of her word. The only thing left for him to do was to paint, to try and hide from thoughts of her.

"I am sorry, my friend." Mr. Bingley stood up and came to pat Mr. Darcy on the shoulder in a gesture of comfort.

"Thank you for telling me, all the same," Mr. Darcy said and continued to stare into space until Mr. Bingley left the room.

As soon as Mr. Darcy was alone with his broken heart, he picked up a paintbrush and continued to paint, more furiously this time.

With each stroke, he discovered that painting was a great distraction as it allowed him to drown the tortured thoughts taking over his mind.

He spent the entire day in the studio, with no food. When night started to fall, he finally emerged.

"How are you feeling?" Mr. Bingley asked.

"I feel that I cannot give up. I cannot give up until I get a chance to speak to Elizabeth. If she rejects my feelings, then I will know that it was not meant to be."

"So you want to make sure she really wants to marry the prince?"

"That's exactly what I want to find out."

"Do you plan on returning to the Longbourn house? After what you shared with me last time, I doubt Mrs. Bennet will allow you to enter."

"No, I will not go there. I have another way that would allow me to be alone with Elizabeth without Mrs. Bennet present. But I may need your help with my plan."

Mr. Bingley nodded. "Of course, Darcy. Whatever you need."

Mr. Darcy proceeded to tell Mr. Bingley about his plan, then he had a late dinner and retired to his room.

He was about to take a risk and there was no guarantee that Elizabeth would agree to talk to him at all, especially after how they left things the last time they saw each other. But he had to speak to her or he would regret it for the rest of his life.

He tried to get to sleep but failed. In the end, he gave up and went outside for a walk in the dark with no destination in mind. The more he thought of Elizabeth, the more he regretted not having opened up his heart to her earlier.

He had known for a while that she was the woman for him, and now that she was engaged to another man, his feelings had only intensified.

When he returned back to the house, he found Mr. Bingley in the parlour having a drink. He, too, was being tortured by thoughts of the woman he loved, another Bennet daughter.

Neither of them felt the need to speak as they sat side-by-side, nursing their drinks and broken hearts in silence.

After the silence, Mr. Bingley told Mr. Darcy that he would also make a plan to talk to Jane. Mr. Darcy was glad to hear his friend had found the courage to go after what his heart wanted. Hopefully one of them would end up having their wishes come true.

Mr. Bingley returned to bed, but Mr. Darcy continued on to the studio, where he spent another few hours perfecting the paintings that could change his life."

CHAPTER 13

Two days after Prince Gabriel proposed, Elizabeth met him again for breakfast at the Rosewood Inn. It was no surprise to her that all he talked about during the entire meal was the wedding, and how excited he was at the prospect of making her his wife.

Elizabeth felt terrible that she was struggling to match his excitement. Instead of excitement, she felt overwhelmed at the fact that all everyone spoke about was her upcoming wedding. People in town constantly stopped to congratulate her.

"I look forward to spending the rest of my life with you, Elizabeth." Prince Gabriel's voice drew her back to the present.

Elizabeth gave him a shaky smile.

"My family will absolutely adore you." He took a drink of his tea, his eyes fixed on her face. "Is everything all right? You look unwell."

Elizabeth nodded and lifted her cup of tea to her lips to give herself a moment before she responded to his comment. She must have been silent for too long because Prince Gabriel leaned back and frowned.

"Are you certain you're well? You have that faraway look on your face again."

Elizabeth lowered her teacup to the table, trying hard to keep her hand from shaking. "I apologize. As you know sometimes I disappear into my own thoughts."

"It is something I find myself needing to grow accustomed to." Prince Gabriel's face grew serious.

Watching him, Elizabeth felt her heart shrink. As much as she did her best to deny it, his proposal had changed something. Suddenly, it was as if she felt she could no longer be quite herself around him. While they had been friends getting to know each other, she'd been more open and was able to enjoy the same things he did, to hold long conversations that both inspired and satisfied her. But ever since she agreed to be his wife, she felt different. No matter how much she tried, she was certainly not as excited as a bride-to-be should be.

In fact, last night, she had requested of her mother that there should be no more wedding preparations done until she met Prince Gabriel's family, that the wedding did not have to happen so soon. She had told the prince as much and he, too, seemed rather disappointed and told her that his family would not mind not being as involved in the preparations.

Mrs. Bennet was horrified that Elizabeth would even make such a suggestion. Elizabeth's wedding was another chance for her mother to stand out, to be the proud mother of a future princess. The sooner she set things in motion, the better. She made it clear to Elizabeth that she would continue with her wedding preparations whether Elizabeth was involved or not and that the date would be set within a week. Her mother had even spoken with the prince, and he had assured her that he would return with the special marriage license, allowing them to marry before the banns had been read.

"Tell me more about your family," Elizabeth said. It was best to get him to talk so he wouldn't ask her questions, some of which she did not wish to answer.

"I'd be glad to tell you more about your future family," Prince Gabriel said, the smile returning to his lips.

As he spoke, Elizabeth sank back into her thoughts, daydreaming about nothing in particular. From a distance, she heard Prince Gabriel telling her stories about his sister and how it was to be raised both in England and France.

The conversation continued until Elizabeth had to return home. Prince Gabriel accompanied her to the house.

When they stepped out of the carriage, they were almost knocked over by Kitty, who rushed out of the house to meet them.

"There's a letter for you, Elizabeth." She waved a piece of paper in the air. "It is an invitation. One of the servants brought it home from Meryton."

"Who is it from?" Elizabeth asked. She took the paper from Kitty's hands and frowned down at it while Kitty disappeared back into the house without giving her an answer.

For no reason whatsoever, Elizabeth took a few steps away from the prince, so he would not see the letter.

She did not wait until she entered the house to read it.

My dearest Elizabeth,

It is been a while since we met. I would love and appreciate the pleasure of your company at the Meryton gallery on Wednesday at noon. I do wish you can make it. For now, I shall be looking forward to seeing you again after so long.

Yours kindly,

Daisy Fields

Staring at the letter, Elizabeth wondered who Daisy Fields was. No matter how thoroughly she searched her mind, she was unable to recall being acquainted with someone of that name. But clearly the person knew her.

"Good news, I hope," Prince Gabriel said as Elizabeth folded up the letter.

"It is from a good friend of mine." She

glanced down at the folded letter in her hands. "She has requested I meet her at the Meryton gallery in two days."

Even though Elizabeth had always prided herself on being truthful, she had just lied to the man she was about to marry. She still had no idea who Daisy Fields was, and she could have said as much to Prince Gabriel, but she did not. She hated that she was becoming a version of herself that she was not fond of.

Prince Gabriel approached her and kissed her hand. "Since I have decided to extend my stay, I would be honored to accompany you to the gallery."

Elizabeth shook her head quickly. "That's not necessary. She is an old friend and we have not seen each other for quite some time. I am afraid we will speak at length about topics unlikely to interest you. I would not like you to get bored."

Prince Gabriel was silent for a moment, his face expressionless. Then he nodded and smiled. "Very well, then. I guess I shall see you in the morning."

Mrs. Bennet had insisted that Prince Gabriel come and have breakfast with them tomorrow. Speaking of Mrs. Bennet, it surprised Elizabeth that her mother did not come out to speak to the prince before he left. He was only dropping her off but Mrs. Bennet never missed a chance to get close to her future son-in-law.

Elizabeth remembered her saying that she would be going with Lady Lucas to Meryton. Perhaps she had already left.

"See you in the morning." Elizabeth waved at Prince Gabriel as he got back in the carriage. There was still a tense look on his face that made her fear that he knew something of her deception.

As she watched the carriage disappear into the distance, she felt guilty for having lied to him about Daisy Fields. For her to do such a thing, something had to be wrong with her. As his future wife, she should have been excited to have him by her side, to introduce him to her friends. Instead she chose to lie about someone she did not even know.

Elizabeth finally went into the house, where Kitty asked who Daisy Fields was. She was not surprised that Kitty had read her letter before she delivered it. She had always been an insatiably curious person.

"She is an old friend, that's all." Elizabeth was unable to stop herself from lying again. However, if she told the truth, Kitty may mention it to the prince when he came for breakfast, and he would know Elizabeth had lied to him.

Kitty frowned. "Why is she inviting you to the gallery?"

"Because we both enjoy art and we haven't seen each other in a while."

"Would you be taking the prince?" Lydia asked, coming out of one of the rooms to join them.

"Unfortunately not. He will be occupied on that day."

As she spoke, Elizabeth thought perhaps it wasn't such a bad idea for her to go out on her own. Being away for some hours would give her a break from the wedding preparations. It would give her a moment to breathe, to be alone. She did not even care much who Daisy Fields was. Visiting the gallery would do her good either way.

But before night fell, she felt so guilty about having lied to Prince Gabriel that she confided in Jane, but only after making her promise to not breathe a word to anyone.

"What a mysterious letter." Jane said. "I cannot wait for you to find out who this Daisy Fields is."

"Neither can I. Honestly, it would give me a chance to get away from mother's talk of the wedding."

"Are you not excited about your wedding?" Jane asked as she braided Elizabeth's hair.

Elizabeth hesitated. "Of course I am, but you know Mama. She can get carried away sometimes."

"I know exactly what you mean." Jane picked up the brush. "Lady Lucas was here for breakfast and they discussed flower arrangements for an entire hour."

"That's exactly what I mean." Elizabeth laughed in spite of herself.

"Would you like me to come with you to the gallery when you go and meet Daisy Fields?" Jane asked, but Elizabeth thanked her and declined the offer, just as she had done with Prince Gabriel.

"I shall be fine alone," she said.

CHAPTER 14

❦

The day before Elizabeth was to meet Daisy Fields, she and her sisters decided to spend as much time together as possible because soon Lydia would return back to Mr. Wickham to continue her confinement at home and Elizabeth would eventually move to France.

As soon as Prince Gabriel left, shortly after breakfast, the four sisters went out into the garden for a long walk and spoke of the fun they used to have as children. It saddened them that Mary was not there to complete them. It also felt strange for Elizabeth to think of Lydia as a wife and soon-to-be mother. Each time she looked at her sister, she still saw the face of the little girl she used to know. But Lydia had clearly matured, and she was excited about the idea of becoming a mother in only a few months, even though she admitted that she was terrified of the birthing process and wished the baby could show up in another way without all the pain.

"Once you see your baby, it will all be worth it," Kitty said, giggling. "We cannot wait to hold her or him."

The Bennet sisters continued to enjoy each other's company as they returned to the house and Jane commented on how quiet it was.

"It won't be long before the sound of a baby crying is heard in this house," Elizabeth said, touching Lydia's stomach.

Lydia placed a hand over Elizabeth's. "Who knows, Lizzy, by this time next year, you could be the one expecting a little one of your own."

Elizabeth gently withdrew her hand and forced a smile. This was a conversation she was not ready to have right now, especially since the wedding had yet to happen. Her mother had made a similar comment last night at supper, excited at the idea of her grandchildren being royalty.

The more her mother talked about

Elizabeth becoming a part of the royal family and how it would change all their lives, it became harder for Elizabeth to hide her discomfort. Of course she did not blame her mother for being excited about marrying off yet another daughter. It was, after all, any mother's dream. Yet, she could not help how she felt.

That day, Elizabeth hid her discomfort well and did her best to join in the conversation before her sisters figured out that something was amiss. They all giggled like little girls as they enjoyed a picnic together in the garden for lunch. They remained outside until Mr. and Mrs. Bennet returned to the house after visiting friends.

Later in the afternoon, when Lydia was having a nap and Kitty was reading a book in the library, Jane and Elizabeth went on another walk. Elizabeth had been watching Jane all day and sensed that she was not completely herself. Her suspicions were confirmed even more since Jane hardly said a word during their walk.

"Are you all right, Jane?" Elizabeth took Jane's hand when they reached the stables.

"Of course I am. Why do you ask?" Jane turned to face her.

"It is just that you're rather quiet."

"You're right." Jane reached out to touch Elizabeth's cheek. "I was thinking about your wedding. It occurred to me that once you're married and gone I would be the old maid in the Bennet household." She shrugged. "Who knows, Kitty could be the next one getting married, then it would be just me." Jane's eyes filled with tears that she blinked away.

"Oh, Jane." Elizabeth pulled her into her arms and held her for a while before pulling back. "With your beauty and intelligence, any man would be happy to have you for a wife. The right man for you will show up before you know it."

"Indeed, any man would be happy to have me, except Mr. Bingley." A bittersweet smile formed on Jane's lips as she crossed her arms in front of her chest. "He did not feel I was good enough for him."

"Then he was blind," Elizabeth said. She considered telling her sister why Mr. Bingley had stayed away, but she could not find the courage. It might upset her even more that Mr. Bingley could be swayed so easily by another's opinion.

"Lizzy, I must admit to hoping, that since he is in town, he would come for a visit, especially given that I have told Mr. Darcy that I would welcome a visit."

"It could be that he is busy. He might call upon you before he leaves." Elizabeth wished so much she could find the words to heal Jane's broken heart.

"I doubt it. It is not me he came back for. It is best for me to come to terms with it."

Elizabeth placed her hands on Jane's shoulders. "Do not be upset. It is better to marry the right person than the wrong one. Do not feel the need to rush into a marriage. Your prince will arrive when the time is right."

"So I should just enjoy the wait? Is that what you're saying?"

"That's exactly what you should do. You should not feel you need a man to be content."

"But what if my prince never comes?" Jane's voice was almost a whisper.

"You cannot think like that," Elizabeth said sternly. "Believe me, he will come."

Jane nodded and did not say anything more. In silence they fed the horses and enjoyed the soft breeze sweeping through their hair. When the silence stretched on for too long, they talked about Lydia's baby, and then to Elizabeth's disappointment, Jane changed the subject to Elizabeth's wedding.

"I am so happy for you, Lizzy. I truly am. You deserve the best. Please tell me that you're no longer having doubts. Sometimes I sense that you're not that excited about the wedding."

"Maybe you're right. When it comes to weddings, there's just so much to think about. It can be overwhelming. Sometimes I wish I could have a simple wedding instead."

"Well, stop wishing. Mama would never agree to a small wedding, not when you're marrying a prince."

"You are right about that." Elizabeth laughed. "Do not worry about me, Jane. Of course I am excited about the wedding even when I do not show it."

"And are you excited about Prince Gabriel?" Jane raised an eyebrow. "Or does Mr. Darcy still occupy your mind?"

"Goodness, no. I no longer pay him any thought." Elizabeth looked down at her hands. "Prince Gabriel is a wonderful man. He will make a good husband."

"Then do not push him away," Jane said. "He cares for you deeply. I do not doubt he will be affectionate with you even after marriage."

Elizabeth nodded and said nothing.

"I will miss you dearly when you move to France, Lizzy."

"And I will miss you." Elizabeth hugged Jane. "But you will visit, won't you? We shall beg Prince Gabriel to cover the cost of travel."

Prince Gabriel had not yet brought up the topic of whether he intended for him and Elizabeth to live in France after the wedding, but Elizabeth knew it was only a matter of time before they discussed plans for the future.

"Of course I will." Jane stepped back and squeezed Elizabeth's hands. "I would not miss the chance to visit another country." Jane looked back at the house. "I think we should get back. It looks as though it will rain any minute."

"Yes, we should." Elizabeth gazed up at the cloudy sky, which was pregnant with rain.

There was no more talk of the wedding as they returned to the house, but as soon as the door opened, Mrs. Bennet rushed up to Elizabeth with swatches of fabric, asking her which one she preferred for the table covers. Elizabeth reached out and chose one without giving it much thought. Mrs. Bennet did not even seem to notice as she returned to her sewing room. She prided herself in her sewing skills and wished to display them by creating items for the wedding.

Before dinner, Mr. Bennet asked Elizabeth to join him in the library.

"I have been meaning to speak to you," he said, asking her to sit down. "But I never got a moment alone with you."

"What's going on, Papa? Is everything all right?"

Mr. Bennet leaned forward and held her gaze. "That's the exact same question I want to ask you."

"I do not understand." Elizabeth found herself tensing up inside. "What do you wish to know?"

"If you're indeed happy." He touched her cheek. "That's what I'd like to know."

She frowned at the question, the same one he had asked after the proposal was first accepted. Elizabeth was unable to speak for a while as she tried to remember the answer she had given Jane when they were at the stables.

Mr. Bennet broke the silence. "I feel the need to ask because your mother has been taking over your wedding. I was concerned that you might find it overwhelming."

Elizabeth smiled, a quiet relief fluttering in her stomach. "Do not worry, Papa. We both know how Mama is. And she has the right to be excited about the wedding."

"How about you?" He lowered his voice. "Are you still excited about marrying the prince?"

Elizabeth was tempted to tell her father the truth of how she felt, but she resisted the urge. She could not tell anyone, not even the people closest to her. "Prince

Gabriel is a good man. I am honored that he chose me for a wife. I *am* excited about the wedding."

The way Mr. Bennet looked at Elizabeth made her feel as though he could see right through her. Maybe she did not even need to say a thing for him to know the truth.

It would all be all right, she told herself. She would get over her discomfort once she and the prince were married and had started a life together.

"Just promise me one thing, my dear girl," Mr. Bennet said.

"Anything for you, Papa."

"You know I want what's best for you. I need you to promise me that you will always be honest about the things that truly make you happy." He shook his head. "There are enough miserable people in the world and you were not born to be one of them. I was sure of it the moment I saw your little face for the first time."

Elizabeth allowed her father's words to sink into her heart before she spoke. "It means a lot to me. I promise, Papa."

"Good. But also promise me that you will marry for love. Only enter into a marriage you know is the right one for you." Mr. Bennet scratched his beard. "Not too long ago, you refused to marry Mr. Collins because your heart knew he was not the right husband for you. I do hope that this time you will also follow your heart."

"I will." Elizabeth blinked away the tears welling up in her eyes.

"I need a promise, Elizabeth Bennet." Mr. Bennet's expression grew even more serious.

Elizabeth waited a few heartbeats, then forced a smile. "I promise."

"Very well." Mr. Bennet lifted himself from his chair. "Now, you'd better go to your mother. I can hear her calling for you. I am sure it is something to do with the wedding. She speaks of nothing else."

Elizabeth stood up and walked to the door. Before she could leave, she turned to her father. "Papa, you never told me how you feel about Prince Gabriel. You do not talk much about him at all, in fact."

"Lizzy, even though I gave him my blessing, how I feel about him is not as important as how you feel about him. You will be the one spending the rest of your life by his side."

Elizabeth nodded. "Did you ever have doubts before marrying Mama?"

"Your mother can be unbearable at times, but when I made the choice to marry her, it was my choice alone. And that's a choice I get to live with for the rest of my life and I do not regret it. I wish for you that you make the right one." He sighed. "You value your freedom too much to enter into a marriage that would feel like a trap."

Elizabeth forced a smile, then opened the door and walked out to go and prepare for her wedding, even when her mind refused to let go of thoughts related to Mr. Darcy. At the back of her mind she feared she felt more for him than she was allowing herself to believe. But how could her feelings for him change so suddenly?

By the time she arrived in the kitchen, where Mrs. Bennet awaited her, she had pushed any thoughts she had about Mr. Darcy to the back of her mind. She reminded herself that she had no right to entertain thoughts of one man while engaged to another.

CHAPTER 15

"Are you sure you do not want me to come with you to the gallery?" Jane asked as she watched Elizabeth getting dressed.

"Quite sure," Elizabeth said. She still did not know, after two days, who Daisy Fields was, but getting out of the house and away from her mother would be a relief. The pressure was becoming too much for her and she was finding it hard to breathe. She had to get out of the house, to have time to herself and enjoy some art with no talk of weddings to interrupt her. She turned to look at Jane. "Papa will be going to Meryton as well. I will have him for company on the way there and back."

"In that case, I will see you later." Jane kissed Elizabeth on both cheeks and disappeared from the room.

Dressed and ready to go, Elizabeth was about to leave the room when Mrs. Bennet appeared in the doorway. "Lizzy, where in the world are you going?"

"To Meryton, to visit the gallery."

"You cannot do that." Mrs. Bennet folded her arms across her chest. "There's so much for you to do around here. Mrs. Daniels will be arriving soon to talk about the wedding cake. We shall have cake, plenty of it. It's a royal wedding after all."

"Who is Mrs. Daniels?" Elizabeth asked.

"She is the best baker in the whole of Hertfordshire. And she has agreed to bake your wedding cake. She does not pick just anybody, you know. In fact, she was booked out." Mrs. Bennet clutched Elizabeth's arm. "But since we will be having a royal wedding, she has decided to make an exception."

"Oh, yes," Elizabeth exclaimed. "I have heard of her delicious cakes."

Mrs. Bennet's face broke into a smile. "I am sure you have. She will make the most magnificent cake for your wedding."

"But how about the cost, Mama? Her

baked goods are supposed to be rather expensive."

Mrs. Bennet placed her hands on Elizabeth's cheeks. "Do not worry yourself, Lizzy. I am sure the prince would not spare any expenses for his bride. He would wish the best for you." Mrs. Bennet paused. "When Mrs. Daniels arrives, make sure to put on your happiest face. She will be here any minute."

Elizabeth shook her head. "I would love to stay, but I have plans, Mama. I *did* mention to you last night that I am going to the gallery today. Remember the invitation I received from my friend?"

"Oh, yes, Daisy something?" Mrs. Bennet murmured.

"Yes, Daisy Fields. She is expecting me at noon and I cannot let her down."

Mrs. Bennet's face tightened. "Well, you have no choice. You have to cancel. I will send one of the servants to deliver a message to her at the gallery."

"No, mother. I will be going."

Elizabeth watched as her mother's face darkened with disappointment. "Elizabeth Bennet, you must show respect for my nerves. I already told Mrs. Daniels that you will be here. She is very excited to talk to a future princess."

"You will have to cancel, Mama. Tell her to come another day, maybe tomorrow."

"That's out of the question. It would be considered bad manners."

Elizabeth stifled a laugh. It amused her that her mother felt it was bad behavior to cancel an appointment and yet she expected Elizabeth to do just that. "I am truly sorry, Mama, but I cannot cancel my appointment."

"If you choose to go anyway, you shall not have the carriage. The horses are in use."

Elizabeth walked past her mother. "I already spoke to Papa and he offered me the carriage. In fact, he will be accompanying me to Meryton."

"He will be going with you to the gallery?" Mrs. Bennet's face reddened.

"He won't be accompanying me to the gallery, but we will be riding together to Meryton. We will both go to our appointments and meet at the carriage afterwards to return home together."

Mrs. Bennet put a hand to her heaving chest. "The two of you will be the death of me. How could you make plans at such a busy time?"

"I'm afraid it is too late for me to cancel my plans. I trust you to make the right choices for the cake, I know you have wonderful taste, Mama. I look forward to hearing all about it when I return. I should go now." Elizabeth knew that even if she stayed to meet Mrs. Daniels, her mother would be the one doing all the talking anyway, and her preferences would take precedence. So far, it was Mrs. Bennet who was making most of the decisions, and it concerned Elizabeth how little that mattered to her.

As Elizabeth walked away to let her father know that she was ready to leave, Mrs. Bennet called after her in a sharp tone. She was unable to stop Elizabeth and Mr. Bennet as they got into the carriage and drove off as she watched after them, wagging her finger.

Mr. Bennet chuckled. "We better be prepared for the tongue lashing we will get when we return."

"Yes, we had better." Elizabeth could not hold back the giggles that erupted from her.

"Are you excited to be meeting your friend at the gallery?" Mr. Bennet asked Elizabeth when the laughter had died down.

"I am. And it would be nice to look at some paintings. I always find the gallery to be so peaceful."

"So do I. I wish I could join you, but there are matters I must settle with the solicitor. I wish you a nice time." Mr. Bennet leaned back and closed his eyes. "It will do you good to get away for a while."

"Thank you, Papa." Elizabeth was grateful to have a father who understood her so well.

During the ride, Elizabeth and Mr. Bennet did not mention the wedding or the prince once. Instead they spoke about books, music, and travels.

Content, Elizabeth leaned her head against her father as their carriage rocked back and forth on its way to Meryton. She felt so much lighter than she had been at the house.

When they arrived in Meryton, there was still plenty of time left before Elizabeth had to meet Daisy Fields at the gallery. While her father went about his business, she decided to spend her time at Mrs. Brown's Tea shop, a place she used to frequent with her sisters, but had not visited for quite some time. She had brought a book with her to read while she waited for time to pass.

"Miss Bennet, it is good to see you again. You used to come here so often, but now you must be awfully busy." Mrs. Brown, the tea shop owner approached her, a bright smile on her lined, round face.

"I shall always return, Mrs. Brown. Your tea shop is like home to us."

Mrs. Brown beamed at Elizabeth's words. "I have heard wonderful things about your upcoming wedding," she said as she served Elizabeth her tea.

"From my mother, I assume." Elizabeth smiled back.

"Yes. How exciting it all must be. Your mother is so very proud of you for choosing such a rich and handsome man." She took a breath. "It is hard to imagine that one of us is marrying a prince. How are the wedding plans going?"

Elizabeth smiled. "Perfectly. My mother has everything under control."

Everything was indeed going according to her mother's plans. She was getting everything she wanted up to the last detail.

"I am glad to hear that. Your mother must be very busy at this time."

"She is. She hardly takes a break. But I have never seen her happier."

"I have known her for a long time and she can get very excited. But it is understandable. She has been waiting a long time for you girls to get married. It is a shame how Lydia got married, but at least she found someone."

Elizabeth nodded and flipped open her book. She hoped the gesture would serve as a signal for Mrs. Brown to leave her alone to read. But Mrs. Brown sat down across from her and continued to go on about the wedding.

Elizabeth's heart sank. She had come looking for an escape from anything to do with the wedding and now she was stuck with a woman who was known for spreading gossip. Mrs. Brown was clearly trying to get all the details about the wedding from her.

It was a good thing Elizabeth had not brought Prince Gabriel to her tea shop when they visited Meryton together.

Elizabeth was sure that whatever she told Mrs. Brown was sure to be passed on by nightfall.

"I've heard your wedding will be in the papers."

"Is that so?" Elizabeth lifted her cup to her lips and took a sip. "It is the first time I am hearing of it."

"Of course it will be well-publicized. It is not every day that royalty comes to town. Your mother has already contacted all the local papers." Mrs. Brown patted the tight bun on top of her head. "Elizabeth, your wedding is sure to be the talk of town for quite some time. You must be so very excited."

No, Elizabeth was tempted to say, but she just smiled and bit her tongue. They would never understand that instead of excited, she felt claustrophobic.

She decided that the best thing to do in

that moment was to share as little information as possible. Hopefully when Mrs. Brown figured out she was not getting anything out of her, she would get the message and leave.

Mrs. Brown continued to talk about the wedding, oblivious to the fact that Elizabeth was no longer paying her any attention, but instead reading her book.

"Elizabeth," Mrs. Brown leaned forward after a while, "Does your prince happen to have any brothers?"

Mrs. Brown's daughter, Sarah, was older than Jane by at least four years, and she was still unmarried. She had been in love, once, with her childhood sweetheart, but he died tragically two weeks before they were to be married. For years she had closed off her heart, so no other suitors had a chance to win her over. When she finally healed from the heartbreak, there were no more men interested in marrying her. Heartbroken for her, Elizabeth had always prayed that one day she would find another man to love.

"I am afraid he doesn't have any brothers, Mrs. Brown." Elizabeth closed her book because she could not concentrate anyway. "He only has a sister."

Mrs. Brown's shoulders visibly sank. "That's a shame. I had hoped my Sarah will finally get another chance. If your prince had brothers, I am sure your mother wouldn't have minded introducing her to one of them."

"I am so sorry, Mrs. Brown." Elizabeth hated seeing the broken look on the older woman's face.

"There's nothing one can do." Mrs. Brown leaned forward. "Does he perhaps have cousins?"

"I think so, but I have not met them yet… or any other family members."

Mrs. Brown reached out and gripped Elizabeth's hands tight. "If there are any good men among those cousins, would you arrange for Sarah to meet them? I would be forever grateful to you."

Elizabeth swallowed hard and tried to move her hands from the woman's grip, but she was surprisingly strong. "I will try," she said, hoping that would be enough for now.

"You are a lovely girl, Elizabeth. I

always knew that. You have a good heart. Your mother did well raising you."

"Thank you, Mrs. Brown."

Finally, Mrs. Brown stood up and Elizabeth finished her tea in peace.

Not long after, Elizabeth said goodbye as it was close to noon and she had to get to the gallery.

As she neared the gallery, an overwhelming sense of ease swept through her. She had no idea why, but the closer she got, the easier it was for her to breathe. When she reached the door, she drew in a deep breath and pushed it open.

She was surprised that the place was empty, with not a soul present. There had always been people around whenever she'd come before.

As she stood by the door wondering where in the world everyone was, a black-haired woman she had never seen before walked up to her with a warm smile.

"Are you by any chance Daisy Fields?" If she *was* Daisy, Elizabeth knew she had never seen her before, let alone started up a friendship.

"No," the woman said. "But she is

expecting you. Have a look at the paintings while I inform her of your arrival."

"Thank you," Elizabeth said, and the woman walked away. Elizabeth had a feeling that something was not right, but she couldn't place her finger on it.

The only thing she could do was wait to find out what awaited her.

CHAPTER 16

Mr. Darcy's brow was covered in sweat as he paced around his paintings. With a small brush he tried to perfect each of them. But he couldn't make them better if he tried. They were absolutely hideous, even if he said so himself.

"Settle down, Darcy, they are not that bad." Mr. Bingley stood back to observe one of them. "They're quite... unique actually."

"You're only trying to flatter me." Mr. Darcy pulled out a handkerchief to dab at the sweat on his face.

"Not at all. You have put so much work into them. I do hope your plan will be successful."

Mr. Darcy stopped pacing and came to a halt in front of his friend. "What am I doing here?"

Mr. Bingley frowned. "What do you mean?"

Mr. Darcy pointed to the paintings. "I mean, this is utter madness. This is not the person I am."

"You're drunk with love, my friend. Love makes us do things we wouldn't normally do." Mr. Bingley placed a hand on Mr. Darcy's shoulder. "You should be proud of yourself. You are following your heart. That's something many men do not have the courage to do, including myself, if I may add."

"I have nothing to be proud of." Mr. Darcy massaged his brow. "I tricked Elizabeth into coming here."

Mr. Bingley let out a low chuckle. "I have to admit it is not one of your best ideas, but you did what you felt was right. Now you just have to finish what you started."

Mr. Darcy shook his head. "No, I cannot do it. It is wrong."

"So what are you planning to do? Do you intend on picking up the paintings and returning them to Netherfield?"

"That's exactly what I am thinking of doing." Mr. Darcy stormed toward some boxes in the corner of the room and started putting away the brushes and paints. "Elizabeth has made her choice. I have to accept that it is too late for me."

A knock on the door startled both of them. Miss Beatrix Clarke, the gallery owner's niece who was in charge while her aunt was out of town, opened the door. "Mr. Darcy, your guest is here."

Mr. Darcy blanched and tightened his grip on the brush he was holding.

"Should I give her permission to enter?" The woman continued. "Or do you plan on bringing some of the paintings out for her to have a look at? She is already inspecting some of the displays."

"No." Mr. Darcy said after a long time. "I shall show her the paintings inside here."

He stood back to assess his paintings once more, his heart clenched tight beneath his chest. It was indeed too late. Too late for him to back out without looking like a coward. Elizabeth was here, and he was not about to embarrass himself by being weak. He had already come this far to give up now.

"Did she seem at all suspicious?" he asked.

"Not at all. She said she was here to meet Miss Daisy Fields." Miss Clarke answered, as a frown bent her brow.

Mr. Bingley couldn't help chuckling as he walked up to the window.

"Mr. Bingley, I think you should go out there and occupy her while I prepare myself."

Mr. Bingley turned around to face Mr. Darcy. "Only if you promise not to run."

Mr. Darcy smiled in spite of himself. "You have my promise."

When Mr. Darcy was left alone in the back room of the gallery, he stood in the center of the room, his heart thumping as he studied his paintings for the last time before Elizabeth saw them.

Finally, he moved to the window and threw it open to fill his lungs with the invigorating fresh air. He had to gather up his courage. Whatever the outcome, he would deal with it. Right now, he had to do what he came here for, what he spent days planning.

He quickly arranged the paintings on various easels in the order he had planned her to see them. But he covered up the last one because it was the one that would decide his destiny.

Once he finished displaying the paintings, he sat down in a chair to collect himself and his thoughts, and choose the words he was going to say. He hoped Elizabeth would look beyond the ugliness of the paintings to understand the underlying meaning.

Mr. Bingley returned to the back room to ask if he was ready and if she should bring Elizabeth.

"I do not think I will ever be ready." Mr. Darcy rubbed his hands together. "How is she?"

"She is beautiful. I still cannot believe that you did not find her attractive at the Meryton Ball."

"I did not know her then. And a man is allowed to change his mind, isn't he?"

"Of course." Mr. Bingley was quiet for a moment and Mr. Darcy knew why. His thoughts were elsewhere, with Jane

Bennet.

Mr. Darcy promised himself that once his own issues were sorted out, he would do whatever it took to make things right between his friend and the woman he loved. "Did Elizabeth ask what you are doing here?" he asked Mr. Bingley.

"She did. She was certainly suspicious. I told her it was the paintings that brought me here. I did not tell her that you are Daisy Fields." He smiled. "But I did mention that I knew who Miss Daisy Fields was. It is your turn to finish what you started."

Mr. Darcy blew out a breath. "I am sure she will hate the paintings."

"It does not matter. The message behind them is clear and perfect. It is genius, Darcy. If everything goes well, you shall have everything you've ever wanted."

"I should hope so. I have tried for so long to deny that Elizabeth was what I wanted. I can no longer do that. I am ready. Please bring her to me."

The time it took for Elizabeth to come to the room felt like a lifetime. In fact, it felt like a lifetime that Mr. Darcy had been waiting for her to arrive in his life. There had been many obstacles in the way and still one major one that had to be overcome, but he had no doubt in his mind that in spite of their differences, they were meant for each other.

He could hear her voice now from a distance, soft, gentle, and confident. She was the woman for him. She was skilled at challenging him and making him think deeply. He loved the fact that Elizabeth Bennet was not the kind of woman who agreed with whatever anyone said simply because of their status.

Her voice was louder now and so were her footfalls as they reached the door. In anticipation, Mr. Darcy listened to her asking Mr. Bingley questions to which only he had answers.

As the doorknob turned, he placed himself in the middle of the room and waited for her to enter. He was both terrified and excited about her reaction at seeing him. And when the door opened, and she did, her eyes widened.

"Mr. Darcy?" She breathed, turning to look at Mr. Bingley as though he could explain the situation. "I have to say I found it rather suspicious to see you here, Mr. Bingley. You made no mention of Mr. Darcy being here as well."

"Good afternoon, Miss Bennet," Mr. Darcy cut in. "It is good to see you again. How have you been?" When Elizabeth did not respond to his greeting, Mr. Darcy glanced at Mr. Bingley for support.

"Miss Bennet," Mr. Bingley said, "I believe Mr. Darcy has something important to tell you. I shall leave you both alone." Mr. Bingley gave Mr. Darcy a curt nod of farewell and stepped out of the room.

Mr. Bingley left the door open but both he and Miss Clarke retreated towards the entry to the gallery. Mr. Darcy felt that everything was about to change for him, for better or for worse, he was unsure. But the truth remained that he wouldn't leave the room at the back of the gallery the same man.

CHAPTER 17

At the sight of Mr. Darcy, Elizabeth felt the blood draining from her face. She had hoped never to see him again and tried so hard to banish him from her mind. Now there he was in front of her. Her heart raced with hope, a traitor to her mind.

Her gaze moved from his face to his hands. He was holding a brush, stained with white paint. Her eyes locked with his again, and tense silence filled the space between them.

"Miss Bennet," he said finally, running a hand through his hair. She watched as the locks lifted then fell back into place. "I can understand if you are upset but—"

"Mr. Darcy," Elizabeth said, cutting him off, "what are you... what are you doing here?" What was he doing at the gallery, and on a day she was meant to be there? And why was he in the back room? Normally, visitors were not allowed entry. Imagine her surprise when she was told to go there, by Mr. Bingley no less. She had been surprised to see him as well, but not as shocked as she was at seeing Mr. Darcy.

Something was going on and her heart was already racing in reaction to it.

"Mr. Bingley was right. I do have something important I want to say to you."

Elizabeth frowned. "I am afraid I do not have time for conversation. I am supposed to be meeting someone here."

Mr. Darcy's gaze did not waver as he pushed back his shoulders. A small smile fluttered at the corners of his lips. "I am that someone."

"No," Elizabeth said, sighing. "I was invited here by a woman, a friend of mine." She brought her hands to the front of her body and clasped them, in need of something to do. She looked past Mr. Darcy, in hopes to see the unknown friend of hers.

"Does that friend happen to be Miss Daisy Fields?" Mr. Darcy asked.

Elizabeth raised an eyebrow. "You know of her?"

"Indeed, I do. I know her quite well, in fact."

"Is she a friend of yours as well?"

Mr. Darcy took a few steps toward Elizabeth. "I am her." He scratched his beard. "By that I mean, she is my creation."

"Your creation?"

"Yes, Miss Bennet. Daisy Fields exists only inside my mind."

"I do not understand." Elizabeth folded her arms in front of her chest. "Mr. Darcy, I am in no mood for games."

"But why?" A smirk touched his lips. "Games can be vastly entertaining."

Elizabeth let out a laugh. "Those words sound strange coming from you, Mr. Darcy. I never pegged you to be someone who finds games amusing."

"I am a surprise even to myself these days. I have been doing things I wouldn't normally do." He glanced behind him and Elizabeth followed his gaze, her heart fluttering too much for her liking.

"Mr. Darcy, what are you talking

about?" Whatever Elizabeth wanted to say next died on her lips when her mind registered what she was seeing in the various paintings behind Mr. Darcy.

"That is what I am talking about." Mr. Darcy's voice had lowered. "I never considered myself to be a painter, and yet I created those hideous pieces." He laughed, and Elizabeth blinked. There was certainly something different about him. For one, his laughter was quite foreign to her ears.

Surprise stifled any words Elizabeth wished to say next.

"It was me who invited you here, Miss Bennet," Mr. Darcy continued. "I am Daisy Fields. I sent you the invitation."

Elizabeth swallowed hard and moved farther into the room, as though an invisible string was drawing her in. "You lied to get me here?" She did not know how she felt about that. She wasn't even sure she wanted to know.

Mr. Darcy bowed his head, then looked up again. "I had feared that if you knew it was me inviting you, you would not have come."

"So you chose deception instead?"

Elizabeth's voice was barely a whisper. Why had Mr. Bingley not said something? Perhaps Mr. Darcy had asked him to cover up his lies. Elizabeth felt betrayed by both of them.

"I do agree that I should have been honest, but I do not apologize for getting you to come here," Mr. Darcy said from behind her. "I have been wishing to talk to you for quite some time now. There was much left unsaid the last time we were together." He cleared his throat. "*I* left a lot unsaid."

Elizabeth thought back to the last time they had spoken, and the back of her throat ached when she remembered how angry she had been at his behaviour. She had not been interested in what he'd had to say, but she felt now she had no choice but to hear him out. Indeed, her heart insisted she listen. She neared one of the paintings, her brow knitted in confusion. "What do all these paintings mean?"

"Sometimes words fail me." Mr. Darcy said from behind her. "I had thought, or hoped really, that the paintings would be able to communicate my intentions better than I ever could. The woman in all of them is you."

Elizabeth turned slowly to face Mr. Darcy. He was closer than she had thought, though not close enough for her to reach out and touch, but enough to make her rather uneasy. "Why would you paint me, Mr. Darcy?"

"Because as I said before, my words had failed me every time I tried to speak with you." He took a step closer and Elizabeth took one back. She was an engaged woman. It was inappropriate of her to be alone in a room with another man, and her head told her to leave immediately, but her limbs refused to obey.

"So you thought pictures would be more effective?" Elizabeth's fingers touched her lips to hide a smile. She did find it hilarious that he had painted her, and the woman in the pictures looked nothing like her.

"As you love art, I thought it wouldn't hurt."

"Well, in that case, allow me to see what your paintings have to say." Elizabeth turned to look back at the first painting, in search of the message Mr. Darcy wished to share with her. "I hope you know that this woman does not resemble me in the least."

She heard Mr. Darcy shift behind her. "It was the best I could do in the short time I had to my disposal."

"You visited my home," she said without thinking, ignoring his answer. She still kept her back turned to him. "My father told me. Why did you come?"

Mr. Darcy came to stand next to her so both of them were gazing at the painting. "I wished to see you."

At his words, Elizabeth's cheeks warmed up. This was not right. Whatever transpired between them was not proper. But why did it feel like it was? And why did she feel so flustered in his presence?

She had previously thought she disliked him, but after what he did for Lydia and Mr. Wickham, and his willingness to embarrass himself by creating such ugly paintings, she was starting to doubt herself.

"Thank you for helping my sister Lydia," she said before she could stop herself. The truth was, if it weren't for him, Lydia's name and their family reputation would be tainted. "I do not understand why you did it when you despise my family so."

"I do not—" He raised his chin. "I did it for you." Although Elizabeth was still not looking at his face, she could feel the touch of his gaze against her cheek.

She was not ready to accept his answer or what it implied. It was best to dismiss it. "Or, could it be that you did it to make things right by Mr. Wickham, after the way you treated him when your father died?"

She turned to him then. The old Elizabeth was making an appearance, the one who had found Mr. Darcy to be unkind and full of himself. For her sanity, she needed to be assured that he hadn't changed. She was unsure how to act around the new version of him.

"You do not know the complete truth, Miss Bennet."

"I think I do," she said. "I know what you did to him, and I think you could no longer live with the guilt. By helping him and Lydia, you wanted to do something that would encourage him to forgive you."

"Things are not always what they seem, Miss Bennet. People do not always tell the truth."

"And you do?" She tilted her head to one side.

"I care to think I am an honest person." His gaze did not waver as he looked into her eyes. His eyes were so intense she felt the urge to look away, but for some reason she couldn't.

The moment was shattered by voices coming from somewhere else in the gallery. Elizabeth forced herself to come back to her senses. "I need to go, Mr. Darcy. It is not right for me to be here. I am an engaged woman." She pushed back her shoulders. "Whatever reasons you had for helping my sister and her husband, I thank you anyway." She took a step back from him and turned away, but before she could walk to the door, he spoke.

"Believe me, Miss Bennet. The things you had heard concerning me and Mr. Wickham were not accurate."

"It is not true then, that you denied him the money your father left him?" Elizabeth felt her anger toward him return. "From what I heard, your father loved him like a son. You should have treated him like a brother."

"And that I did. Whatever decisions I made concerning him were in his own best interest."

Elizabeth shook her head in disbelief. "I apologize if I find that hard to believe."

"I am sure you would, since you took everything you heard as fact." Mr. Darcy approached one of the two windows in the room. "If you would care to hear the truth, and not the version of it that Mr. Wickham had been sharing, I will gladly tell you."

"And what truth is that?" Elizabeth's mind told her to end the conversation, to leave the room, and never look back, but something kept her there.

"If I had given Mr. Wickham the entire fortune my father had left him, he would have gambled it away, the way he had gambled what I had already given him. My refusal to give him more made him a bitter man who would go to great lengths to get revenge. Part of his plan was to elope with my sister, Georgiana, at the tender age of fifteen."

Elizabeth felt her cheeks blush. "I did not know this." As Elizabeth searched his eyes, she could tell he was not lying. Her mind took her back to her conversation with Mr. Wickham, when he told her what Mr. Darcy had done to him. As he'd said the words, he had not once looked her in the eye. And Elizabeth had disliked Mr. Darcy so much that it had been easy to believe every word Mr. Wickham had said about his character.

"It is the truth as I know it. Whom do you believe, Elizabeth? Me or Mr. Wickham, a man who very nearly ruined your youngest sister?"

Elizabeth bit her lower lip. "It does not matter. What you said does not change my opinion of you. You have done other unforgivable things. I cannot forgive you for standing in the way of Mr. Bingley and Jane's happiness."

Mr. Darcy hung his head in shame. "I admit I was wrong. I should not have done what I did. At the time I felt I was doing the right thing. Now I know I made a mistake, and I truly regret my actions. I have even encouraged Bingley to follow his heart, if it lies in your sister's direction."

Elizabeth's eyes widened. She could not

have predicted his response, never expected him to admit he was wrong about anything. His words took her so much by surprise that she was momentarily speechless, and that was unlike her. Like him, she was doing a lot of things out of character these days.

"I appreciate you saying that," she whispered, then cleared her throat and walked back to the first painting. He had clearly invested a lot of time in creating the paintings. The least she could do was acknowledge them properly. "Why do I look so sad in this one?"

"When I saw you last, you looked sad, after you talked to Mr. Collins. I remember thinking that sadness does not suit your eyes."

"Mr. Collins had received a letter that said my father was ill. That was the reason for my sadness, and the reason I returned home with such haste." She forced a smile. "But it turned out that I had no reason to be upset at all. My father was fine. He is perfectly healthy."

"I am glad to hear it," Mr. Darcy said. "When I visited your home, I could tell he was a picture of health."

Elizabeth decided not to continue that topic of conversation. She would not tell him that her mother had lied about her father being ill. She hated for Mr. Darcy to see her mother in an even worse light. But why did she care so much what he thought?

Luckily, he did not pursue the topic and instead showed Elizabeth more paintings of her. She was happy in some and looking lost in others.

She listened attentively and did her best not to interrupt until they reached the last painting that was not covered with a sheet. "That's you, I assume?" In front of her, swathed in paints of various colours and shades, was an unsmiling man trapped in a cage, his lips sealed.

"Indeed, it is me." Mr. Darcy straightened the easel so Elizabeth could see better.

"What does it mean?" As amateur as all the paintings were, Elizabeth found herself unable to look away.

"The reason my lips are sealed is to show my tendency to become speechless in your presence."

Elizabeth placed the tip of her finger on Mr. Darcy's sealed lips. "But you did have plenty to say when we spoke. You had certainly never been speechless around me."

"Miss Bennet, a man can speak a thousand words, but those words do not matter unless they come from his heart." Mr. Darcy took her hand, but she pulled away as soon as she felt the warmth of his skin.

"What are you doing, Mr. Darcy?" She could barely hear her words over the sound of her heart thudding.

"I shall not forgive myself if I let you leave without emptying my heart of the words which make it so heavy." He strode across the room and grabbed a chair. "Please do be seated and listen to what I have to say. After that, I will not ask you to stay if you wish to leave."

Overwhelmed by all she had heard in only a matter of minutes, Elizabeth sank into the chair and braced herself to hear what was on his mind.

CHAPTER 18

 ⌒∞⌒

"Firstly, I would beg your forgiveness for things I did that directly or indirectly hurt you." He inhaled sharply. "Secondly, you should know that I love you, Miss Elizabeth Bennet. It is a truth I am no longer able to keep hidden. If you do not believe a thing I said before now, I beg you to believe these words. I was a fool in the past, but I intend on being a better man in the future."

Someone at the door coughed and both Elizabeth and Mr. Darcy turned to look.

When Elizabeth saw who it was, she got to her feet so quickly she felt faint. Her cheeks were warm as she smoothed down her dress and scrambled inside her mind for something to say to Prince Gabriel, who looked confused and hurt as his gaze moved from her to Mr. Darcy.

"I believe it all makes sense now," he said before she did.

"Prince Gabriel. I—"

"My sister arrived in town this morning." Prince Gabriel no longer looked at either of them as he stepped into the room and approached the window. "She was desperate to meet the woman I planned to marry."

Elizabeth glanced at Mr. Darcy, who gave her a small nod. "I shall leave you alone, if that's what you want, Miss Bennet."

"Yes, please, Mr. Darcy." She wondered how much Prince Gabriel had heard, if he heard anything at all. How long had he been standing there? She could not even imagine how he felt right now.

"I shall return to continue our conversation," Mr. Darcy said and left the room.

Elizabeth walked up to her fiancé and raised a hand to touch his shoulder, but he flinched away from her. She let her hand drop at her side and went to sit down again. So much was changing in her life and she was unsure how to handle all of it at once.

From the way Prince Gabriel looked, it was clear he had heard Mr. Darcy's admission.

"I had no idea your sister was coming," Elizabeth said, gathering her hands in her lap. He had told her a lot about his older sister, Margaret, and Elizabeth had looked forward to meeting her.

Prince Gabriel turned around, his lips thinned with displeasure. "I also did not know she was coming. Her visit was unexpected. Within minutes of her arriving at the inn, she insisted that I come and find you at once."

Elizabeth said nothing, waiting for him to continue. Being around him after Mr. Darcy's revelation felt somehow wrong. She had no idea what to say to him anymore.

"May I ask you a question?" His face grew more serious than she had ever seen it and she detected a muscle in his jaw quivering.

"Yes, yes, of course you may." From the tone in his voice, Elizabeth knew his question could change everything.

"You had told me you were meeting a friend by the name of Daisy Fields. Why did you lie to me?"

"I did not lie to you. I came here expecting to meet her." He still had no idea that Daisy Fields did not even exist. "That is the truth."

"If that is the truth, then why did I..." he inhaled sharply, "why did I find you in here with another man?"

"It was not planned," Elizabeth said quickly. "I had no idea Mr. Darcy would even be here."

"Mr. Darcy," he said the name slowly, as though tasting it on his tongue. Silence fell between them as he moved to the paintings. "Was he the one who painted these paintings?"

"Yes." Elizabeth held her breath, hoping he would not determine the woman in the paintings was her.

Prince Gabriel placed a finger on his lips. "He is not much of a painter, is he? These are terrible."

Elizabeth said nothing. Defending Mr. Darcy's paintings would bring her trouble.

Prince Gabriel turned back to face her. "Tell me, was Mr. Darcy the reason why you ignored me at the Meryton Ball? I had seen you looking at him quite often, if I recall."

Elizabeth was about to speak when she heard what sounded like a squeak. She turned to the door to see a very tall woman—with hair so blonde it looked white—hurry into the room, dressed in a cream and gold gown.

"Margaret, what are you doing here? I asked you to wait at the inn. There was something I needed to discuss with you before—"

"I could find nothing to occupy me," the woman said and approached Elizabeth. She took both her hands in hers, pulling her to her feet. "You must be the beautiful Elizabeth. I have heard so much about you."

Elizabeth swallowed through her dry throat. She was still trying to recover from Prince Gabriel's question.

"My brother's description of you did you no justice at all. You are so much more beautiful in the flesh." Like her brother, her English had no accent to it.

"Thank you. It is lovely to meet you at last." Elizabeth glanced at Prince Gabriel, but he averted his gaze.

"Margaret, I have something important to discuss with Elizabeth. Would you mind giving us a few minutes alone? I won't be long."

Margaret brought her hands together, her face lighting up. "Is it the wedding you wish to discuss?"

Neither Elizabeth nor Prince Gabriel responded.

"Come on, dear brother, your wedding is a family affair, I should be included in the planning. I have many amazing ideas."

Prince Gabriel turned back to the window. "We shall not be discussing the wedding. What we need to talk about is of a private nature."

"Of course, you lovebirds. I understand." Margaret's eyes dance with each word. "I shall give you a moment alone." She grabbed Elizabeth's hand again. "I cannot wait to have you as my sister. I like you already."

After she left, Elizabeth sat down again,

feeling suddenly drained. She did not look forward to continuing the conversation between her and Prince Gabriel.

"Allow me to repeat my question to you," he said. "Was Mr. Darcy the reason why you wouldn't give me a chance at the ball?"

"Prince Gabriel, is this question really necessary?" Elizabeth felt her cheeks warming. "I have accepted your proposal already."

"I think it is, Miss Bennet. Do keep in mind that your hesitancy to answer is an answer in itself. Please tell me the truth. I must know."

"Yes." Elizabeth pursed her lips. There was no point in lying anymore. "You were right in thinking I was distracted by Mr. Darcy. But it was not due to attraction, but from offence. I apologize again for my behavior towards you that evening."

"How about now? Are you still distracted by Mr. Darcy?"

"What do you mean?" She knew exactly what he meant, but she needed to prolong the conversation so she could think of something more appropriate to say to him.

"I always had the feeling every time we were together, you were not present. You were always somewhere else. I brought it to your attention and you assured me time and time again that it would no longer happen. Now I know you were not being honest with me."

"You are right, Prince Gabriel." Elizabeth went to stand next to him by the window. "I should have been upfront with you from the start."

"I agree. But what's done cannot be undone. It is good we had this conversation now rather than later. It is good to know where your heart is."

"My heart—"

A knock on the door startled them both.

Mr. Darcy was standing in the doorway, his eyes on Prince Gabriel. "I apologize for the disturbance, but I was wondering if I could have a word with Miss Bennet. What I have to say cannot wait."

"Of course," Prince Gabriel said. "You actually came at the most appropriate time. Miss Bennet and I have said all there is to say." He turned to her. "Goodbye, Elizabeth. My sister and I will be leaving town tomorrow. You shall not see me again. I wish you much happiness in your life."

He nodded at Mr. Darcy. "I wish you good luck." With that, he walked out without another glance in Elizabeth's direction.

Elizabeth clutched the edge of the windowsill, her face feeling too hot, her eyes damp. She knew she should say something to Prince Gabriel, assure him it was he she wished to spend her future with. But as much as her heart broke for him, it would be a lie. And she was done lying.

If she had to be perfectly honest, she felt like she was right where she needed to be. She'd had doubts from the start of their engagement. She should have been honest to both him and herself then and never let it get as far as it had.

After Prince Gabriel disappeared from the room, her eyes moved to Mr. Darcy's face. "You wished to continue our conversation?"

He nodded. "But it might be best for me to show you instead.

CHAPTER 19

∽

As Mr. Darcy spoke, Elizabeth found herself distracted. She could not even hear the words. Even though she now knew she and Prince Gabriel were never meant to be, she felt terrible for the way she had treated him, the way things had ended. What would her mother say?

How could she possibly move forward with the cloud of his pain hanging in her head? She was not the kind of person who would treat someone so carelessly and just walk away.

She looked back at the door and then at Mr. Darcy, her heart hammering inside her chest.

"Are you well?" he asked, taking a step towards her. "You are upset about what happened, aren't you?"

"Of course I am, Mr. Darcy." Elizabeth swallowed the tears in her throat. "No one deserves to have their heart broken in such a manner."

"Did you love him?" Mr. Darcy asked. "Could you see a future with him?"

"I wanted to." Tears burned the backs of Elizabeth's eyes. "Unfortunately, my heart refused to let me."

"Could it be because another occupied your mind?"

Elizabeth hesitated. Why in the world would he believe that? He could not possibly know that it had been him on her mind while the prince was courting her. "Mr. Darcy, I cannot speak to that when another man is out there brokenhearted."

"I fully understand." He gave a brief nod. "What would you want me to do?"

"It is not you who should do something. I am the source of his heartache." She gathered up her skirt and turned to the door. "I apologize for interrupting whatever you had intended on discussing with me, but I should go after him. I shall never be at peace if I do not explain to him the reasons for calling off the engagement."

"I understand." Mr. Darcy's face took on a serious expression, but his eyes were gentle. Perhaps he feared that Elizabeth would once more walk away without giving him the chance to voice what was on his mind.

Elizabeth gave him a kind smile. "I can assure you that, this time, I will give you a chance to speak your mind." She found it hard to grasp the fact that she did not despise him as much as she thought. She now understood what Lydia had said, about him possibly being a good man even though it did not show on the outside.

"I appreciate that, and I shall wait here for you." Mr. Darcy went to stand by the painting that was covered with a sheet while Elizabeth stood by the door giving him the tiniest of smiles before stepping out of the room.

Her heart felt heavy with each step she took forward. She hoped Prince Gabriel had not already left. If he did, it was a good thing she knew where he stayed. She would ask Papa to accompany her to the Rosewood Inn. It pained her so that she had no idea how she would explain what had happened, or the kinds of words that would offer him consolation. What if whatever she said to him was not enough to numb the pain she had inflicted?

Although she had doubts about the marriage, she had never thought it would end, or that it would end the way it did. Up until she entered the gallery and saw Mr. Darcy, she still believed she was going to be his wife. And now Prince Gabriel would return to France carrying only a broken heart. She could not let him go without attempting to mend what she could.

The moment Elizabeth turned the corner, she saw Prince Gabriel and his sister standing by a window not too far from where she was. Before they could catch sight of her, she hid behind the wall. She used the time in hiding to pull in a few calming breaths and gather up her courage. She had not expected him to still be in the gallery.

As Elizabeth was preparing to reveal herself, their voices drifted towards her. She felt the urge to hear his opinion on what had happened in the hope that she would be better prepared when she faced him again. However, what she heard was far from what she had expected.

"Are you telling me that she actually believed you are a French prince?" Margaret said in a loud enough whisper. "Why would you do such a foolish thing?"

"She would never have given me a chance if she knew I am only a poor farmer's son from Cambridge without a shilling to my name. A woman such as Elizabeth Bennet would want to be married to a wealthy and educated man." Prince Gabriel's voice was heavy with sarcasm. "When I saw her at the ball, I was instantly drawn to her, but she barely paid me any notice. You have to understand that I needed to do something in order to stand out from the crowd."

Elizabeth clutched her chest as she forced herself to breathe. Surely she heard wrong. She strained her ears to catch their next words.

"By going deeper into debt to appear wealthy just so you can con your way into her life? My dear brother, I have to say that's the most despicable thing you have ever done. I do hope you are aware that it was not only her you lied to," Margaret sounded furious. "You fooled the rest of her family, and you lied to me. How could you have been so naïve to think the truth would never reveal itself? When did you even plan on telling her?"

Elizabeth could not believe what she overheard, that Prince Gabriel was not the man she thought he was, that he was not even a prince in the first place. How could that be? How could he have fooled all of them?

She pressed her back against the wall and closed her eyes. Her heart told her to walk away, not to listen to the rest of the conversation because she had heard enough. But shock had rooted her to the spot. It was as though her legs had forgotten how to move and whether she wished it or not, she had no choice but to witness the rest of his shocking confession.

"I am deeply sorry for not being truthful to you, my dear sister. I feel terrible for what I did to Elizabeth, but I did plan on telling her eventually. But I wanted her to fall in love with me first so that when she found out who I truly am, her heart would not give her permission to leave me."

"That's the most ridiculous thing I have ever heard," Margaret said. "Marrying someone under false pretenses would have been a terrible mistake which would have ended in not only her heartache, but yours as well. What were you thinking?"

Prince Gabriel—or whatever his real name was—was silent for such a long time that for a moment Elizabeth thought they had left the gallery. Her eyes fluttered open and she pushed herself away from the wall, but then she heard his voice again.

"I admit I was not thinking fully of the possible consequences. And the only thing I can do right now is offer you my sincere apology for having lied to you."

"Your apology belongs not to me, but to Elizabeth. You owe her the truth. Mother did not raise us this way and if she were alive, you know she would never have condoned your actions."

"That's out of the question. I cannot return to Elizabeth after I found her with another man, a man of great wealth I may add. I have heard people speaking of this

Mr. Darcy around town."

"But she has not given you a reason that she has chosen him." Margaret paused. "You did not witness a proposal, did you?"

"Everything I needed to know was written on her face." His voice was soaked in anger and disappointment. "I have made a fool of myself enough as it is. I'd rather walk away with a part of my dignity intact. Elizabeth Bennet is not the only woman in the world, after all."

"Do not tell me that you plan on carrying on with this foolishness. You will not con another unsuspecting woman."

"I have not decided yet. What I do know is that I have come to appreciate the attention and respect I got as Prince Gabriel. As far as I am concerned, my dear sister, Andrew Harris no longer exists. This is who I am now, the person I was meant to be."

"But—"

"Margaret," Andrew said, cutting his sister off. "I do not wish to discuss this topic further. We should get going. I have packing to do."

As soon as Elizabeth heard their

footsteps and then the sound of the door opening and closing, she pushed away from the wall and stumbled back to the back room of the gallery, her fingers wrapped around her neck as she struggled to breathe.

"Goodness, Miss Bennet, you look a fright," Mr. Darcy said as soon as he saw her. "What in the world happened?"

Elizabeth was unable to speak as she crossed the room towards an empty chair and sank down into it. She dropped her head into her hands and squeezed her eyes shut for a moment. She had to give the words she had heard a chance to sink into her mind in order to be able to share them with someone else.

Even though she could not see him, she could feel Mr. Darcy's presence close by, but he did not pressure her into speaking. She guessed that perhaps he was thinking that the prince had rejected her explanation. If only he knew the truth of what really happened. He would be just as shocked as she was.

After a long moment, she lifted her head and met Mr. Darcy's eyes.

He spoke before she could. "If you would rather not talk about it, I would respect that."

"No." Elizabeth shook her head as tears trickled down her cheeks. The weight of the secret she carried was not one she was willing to bear alone. "But first, I would ask to hear the rest of what you had to say to me before I walked out."

"Are you certain?" Mr. Darcy lifted a hand and looked as though he was about to place it on Elizabeth's shoulder. He changed his mind at the last second, allowing it to drop by his side.

"I am sure, but only if it is something pleasant. I find myself in need of distraction." She gave him a bittersweet smile. "What I have to say would require much more of your time."

Mr. Darcy gave her a hasty nod then approached the covered painting. When he lifted the cover to reveal one of the ugliest paintings Elizabeth had ever seen, she gasped.

"What in the world—" Her weary eyes became instantly clear.

He gave her a sheepish look. "I know it

is horrid, but it was the best I could do."

Giggling in spite of herself, Elizabeth stood up and went to the painting. "And these people are supposed to be a bride and groom?"

"Not just any bride and groom." Mr. Darcy turned her around by the shoulders and gazed into her eyes. "It is you and I, Elizabeth, but only if you would wish it to be. I know that after everything that has happened, this might be too soon, but I have waited so long to tell you these words."

"And what might those words be?" Elizabeth whispered, her eyes filling with tears as she knew exactly what he was about to say.

His gaze still holding hers, Mr. Darcy lowered himself to one knee. "Miss Elizabeth Bennet, what I have been trying and failing so miserably to say to you is that I am very much in love with you, and I would like nothing more than to be your husband."

"Oh, Mr. Darcy." Tears flooded Elizabeth's throat. "I do not know what to say."

"How about a simple yes?" His eyes sparkled as he spoke.

There were times in the past that Elizabeth had thought Mr. Darcy to be cruel. But the one thing she knew about him and now appreciated more than ever was his honesty. He was nothing like the stranger she had almost married, the man who betrayed her.

It made her shiver to think of what could have happened if she never found out the truth, and continued to believe that Gabriel was a good man, not the con artist she now knew him to be. And the truth was, Mr. Darcy had instilled himself in her thoughts and her heart, even when she thought she was going to marry a prince. If she had to be honest with herself, she knew she had fallen in love with Mr. Darcy. She had fought so hard for it to not be so, but she had to admit defeat.

When Elizabeth took too long to give an answer, Mr. Darcy filled the silence. "If you do not wish to accept my proposal, then please accept the paintings as they are too hideous for anyone else to want them."

Elizabeth glanced at the paintings and

then back at Mr. Darcy. "I do want the paintings, but I also want you as my husband." She dropped to her knees and threw herself into Mr. Darcy's arms. It had been him all along and her heart sang with joy.

After Mr. Darcy's proposal, Mr. Bingley came to congratulate them. Then Elizabeth told them both about the fake prince and the con.

Furious, Mr. Darcy threatened to go and find him, to confront him, but Elizabeth stopped him. Andrew was not worth any more of their time, and she believed they should focus on what the future held instead. Mr. Darcy was all too glad to agree with her.

CHAPTER 20

Elizabeth and Mr. Bennet's carriage came to a halt in front of the Longbourn residence, with Mr. Darcy and Mr. Bingley's right behind it.

With both fear and excitement coursing through her veins, Elizabeth turned to her father. "I cannot believe you never told me about Mr. Darcy... that you knew he loved me."

"Marriage is a lifelong commitment, my girl. I wanted you to make a decision that was right for you, not for me."

"I know, Papa, but you could still have told me that you went to see him, and that you saw the paintings."

"Maybe I should have, but I did not want to interfere in your life. Your darling mother meddles enough for the both of us." Mr. Bennet patted her hand. "But I am happy you chose Mr. Darcy. A man who goes to such lengths to win the heart of the woman he loves is the kind I want for my daughter. But the most important thing to me is that you feel so deeply for him in return."

"I do." Tears of joy filled Elizabeth's eyes. "It took a while, but I am where I was meant to be. I do love him, Papa." Her face fell as she remembered what she was about to do. "But how would I explain all this to Mama? She had been so excited about the prince."

"My darling Elizabeth, she will have no choice but to accept your engagement to Mr. Darcy. After all, the prince does not exist. As a matter of fact, he never did." Elizabeth had already told Mr. Bennet what she had overheard, and he had been as furious as Mr. Darcy, but equally as relieved that they discovered the truth early enough. "Do not worry about your mother. I will start the conversation."

Elizabeth glanced out the window to see Mrs. Bennet bouncing out of the house, her face covered in smiles. But she came to an abrupt halt when she caught sight of the second carriage behind theirs.

"We better get out there before she gives Mr. Darcy a tongue lashing." Mr. Bennet opened his door and got out as Mrs. Bennet was making her way to Mr. Darcy and Mr. Bingley's carriage. Mr. Darcy was the first to step out.

"Mr. Darcy," Mrs. Bennet planted her hands on her hips. "I am afraid this is not a good time for visits. We have important wedding preparations to see to."

"It is a pleasure to see you again, Mrs. Bennet." The smile on Mr. Darcy's face showed that he did not mind the words that had been thrown at him.

Mrs. Bennet parted her lips to continue, but she forgot her words when Mr. Bingley exited the carriage.

"Mr. Bingley," she said, dropping her hands from her hips. "How wonderful of you to visit." She ran up to Mr. Bingley, completely ignoring Mr. Darcy. "Your company is always welcome in our home. No need for an invitation." She took Mr. Bingley's arm and led him towards the house before he could change his mind.

As they moved forward, the front door was opened wider and Elizabeth's sisters walked out. Upon seeing Mr. Bingley, Jane froze in the doorway and placed a hand on her lips. The other Bennet sisters looked just as shocked to see the unexpected visitors.

Mr. Bingley released himself from Mrs. Bennet's grip and walked up to Jane. He stretched out his hand towards her. "May I have a word with you, Miss Bennet?" he asked.

Jane hesitated for a moment, peering past his shoulder towards Elizabeth, who gave her a tiny nod and a secret smile. Jane accepted Mr. Bingley's hand and allowed him to escort her on a walk.

Mrs. Bennet looked after them, her hands clasped under her chin, her eyes filled with tears. And then she remembered Mr. Darcy's presence and spun around. "Mr. Darcy, this is truly a dreadful time to visit."

"Mrs. Bennet, no need to be so unkind." Mr. Bennet took his wife's arm and ushered her away. "Mr. Darcy is here with very good news. Let me tell you all about it."

As soon as Mr. and Mrs. Bennet disappeared into the house, Lydia and Kitty rushed up to Elizabeth to ask what was going on.

When Elizabeth told them, they were horrified to learn that the man they had come to know as Prince Gabriel had never existed, and after a moment of surprise, they were overjoyed that Elizabeth still managed to find love in a different man. Especially one so wealthy, Lydia reminded them, but Kitty and Elizabeth admonished her quickly.

While her sisters were still digesting the new information, Elizabeth personally invited Mr. Darcy into their home as Mrs. Bennet had failed to do it.

As soon as Elizabeth, her sisters, and Mr. Darcy gathered in the sitting room, they heard a scream coming from the drawing room—where Mr. Bennet was breaking the news to Mrs. Bennet— followed by the thud of angry footsteps headed in the direction of the sitting room. Mrs. Bennet soon burst into the room and turned on Elizabeth.

"Elizabeth Bennet, please tell me that Mr. Bennet is wrong. Tell me you have not called off the engagement," Mrs. Bennet cried, her face pale with anger.

"He is not wrong, Mama," Elizabeth said. "I shall not be marrying a prince."

Mrs. Bennet's eyes widened with horror. "But why? He is a prince!"

Before Elizabeth could respond, Mr. Bennet walked into the sitting room as well, his face defeated. It was clear that Mrs. Bennet had not given him the chance to tell her the complete story. It was up to Elizabeth to do so before her mother turned on Mr. Darcy again.

She faced her mother again. "Mama, Prince Gabriel was not the man we all thought he was. He is a liar."

"How dare you talk about that lovely young man in such a manner," Mrs. Bennet blanched. She looked about to faint from nerves. Her dream of having her daughter become a princess was collapsing and she was unable to handle it.

"I am telling you the truth, Mama." Elizabeth walked up to Mrs. Bennet and tried to touch her, but she shrank away from her touch. There was no easy way to say the words that needed to be said, so she went ahead and completed the story.

As soon as Elizabeth was done, Mrs. Bennet lost the fight to keep it together and fainted. She was caught by Mr. Bennet before she hit the floor. With the help of Mr. Darcy, he moved her to the sofa. But she came to quickly after Kitty rushed for the smelling salts.

"So he lied to me?" Mrs. Bennet whispered.

Elizabeth knelt down next to the sofa to get to her mother's level. "He did. He lied to all of us."

"So, there will be no wedding?" Mrs. Bennet's damp eyes were panicked as they held Elizabeth's gaze. "We'll be the mockery of the town."

Elizabeth squeezed her hand and quickly told the story of how Mr. Darcy had proposed to her at the gallery.

Mrs. Bennet's gaze swept the room in search of Mr. Darcy. When her gaze settled on him, the corners of her lips twitched. "I apologize for the way I treated you, Mr. Darcy. Especially after everything you have done for Lydia and Mr. Wickham. Deep down I always knew you were a good man, I never allowed myself to believe it because I thought the prince was a better man for my Elizabeth. Certainly you understand I only wanted what was best for my daughter?" Mrs. Bennet's face clouded as she struggled to sit up. "How could someone do such a terrible thing to good people like us?"

Mr. Bennet patted her shoulder. "The good news is that we found out when we did. Now it is best we focus on the future instead of the past."

"I agree," Mr. Darcy added. "And we have a wedding to plan."

All of a sudden, Mrs. Bennet's face cleared and she straightened up, as though she had not fainted at all, the realization clear on her face. "You mean the wedding preparations can continue? Oh, Mr. Darcy, that makes me very happy." She got to her feet and went to grab Mr. Darcy's hands, gazing into his eyes as though he was the most perfect man. "Thank you for everything you have done."

Mr. Darcy smiled back at her. "And

thank you for giving me the permission to marry your daughter."

Mrs. Bennet moved on to Elizabeth and dragged her to where Mr. Darcy stood. "You two belong together. I can already see it." She started to move around the sitting room in excitement as everyone watched her with smiles on their faces. And then she turned back to Elizabeth and Mr. Darcy. "Mrs. Daniels will return tomorrow to discuss the wedding cake. You will be there." It was an order, not a question.

Elizabeth laughed like she hadn't laughed in a long time. Before she could answer, Jane and Mr. Bingley entered the sitting room with smiles on their own faces.

"Make that two wedding cakes, Mama," Jane said. "Mr. Bingley has asked me to be his wife."

"This is too much." Mrs. Bennet said, clutching her chest. "How could I possibly fit so much joy inside my heart? Two daughters engaged!"

"I am certain you will manage, my dear," Mr. Bennet came to her side. "I am guessing there will be lots of bundles of joy coming our way in the near future."

Everyone laughed, and more congratulations were passed around, then with Mrs. Bennet as the leader, the wedding plans commenced in earnest.

This time, Elizabeth was more than happy to be involved.

Both Elizabeth and Jane, as well as their future husbands, confirmed their desire to marry on the same day, and quite soon.

CHAPTER 21

❧

A few days after Elizabeth and Jane got engaged, Mr. Darcy and Mr. Bingley received an invitation to dine with the Bennets.

Mrs. Bennet was so very proud that her two eldest daughters were to be married to men of such high social status. As could be expected, the day before they were to arrive, she was beside herself with excitement and ran around in constant agitation, giving the servants clear instructions and making sure everything was perfect. Her dislike of Mr. Darcy had completely melted away, and that night, while they were preparing for bed, she hinted to Mr. Bennet that he was to be her favourite son-in-law.

"You cannot have favourites, Mrs. Bennet. You shall love them all equally." Upon uttering the words, it occurred to Mr. Bennet that he, too, had a favourite among his daughters. But he assured himself that even though he was closer to Elizabeth, it did not mean he loved his other daughters any less.

"Of course I will love them equally," Mrs. Bennet said, irritated by Mr. Bennet's comment. "All I am saying is that I have come to be quite fond of Mr. Darcy. He has done so much for our family."

"I do agree with that." Mr. Bennet said, making himself comfortable in the bed.

"Tomorrow will have to go perfectly," Mrs. Bennet said, sliding into bed next to her husband. "It will be our first chance to prove to Mr. Darcy and Mr. Bingley that we are a worthy family to be a part of."

"And indeed we are." Mr. Bennet picked up a book and flipped it open. "I am positive they already appreciate us for the simple fact that we will be giving them such beautiful and intelligent daughters to marry."

Mrs. Bennet said nothing more as she drifted into her thoughts, already thinking about the wedding day of her two eldest daughters. The celebrations would take place on the following Sunday, the special licenses having been received, and she had barely been able to sleep while she planned every detail. Both Jane and Elizabeth, as well as their future husbands, appreciated her efforts in the wedding preparations and hardly ever interfered.

"You should sleep," Mr. Bennet said, closing his book. "Tomorrow will be an exciting day."

Mrs. Bennet agreed with him and soon after closing her eyes, she fell asleep, dreaming of her daughters' weddings.

* * *

While their parents slept, all five Bennet sisters gathered in one bedroom to spend as much time together as they possibly could. The time they spent was even more cherished as Mary had arrived from London that morning to be there for the weddings. Her husband, Mr. Sutton, would be joining them the week of the ceremonies as he was currently occupied with a court case.

While Elizabeth would be having her entire family at her wedding, it saddened her that Mr. Darcy would marry without one member of his family present. His aunt, Lady Catherine de Bourgh, had refused his invitation to the wedding as she was heartbroken about his choice to marry Elizabeth instead of her daughter, Anne. She had arrived in Meryton—only two days before—to dissuade Elizabeth from marrying Mr. Darcy, which, of course Elizabeth had refused without question. Infuriated, she had made it known to Mr. Darcy that she would leave town before the wedding happened.

"Lizzy, I still cannot believe you will be marrying Mr. Darcy," Mary cried, pulling Elizabeth out of her thoughts. "We all thought him to be so disagreeable and arrogant."

"Sometimes looks can be deceiving," Elizabeth said, thinking of Mr. Darcy.

The days after he proposed they had spent much more time together, doing the things that she used to do with the prince, and visiting the same places. Even though at first, she had thought she and Mr. Darcy had nothing in common, she was pleased to find that she was in fact wrong. Mr. Darcy appreciated reading as much as she did, even though the subjects he preferred were different to hers. Although he did not appreciate the same kind of art as Elizabeth, they had found a few pieces they both agreed upon and he secured to add to the galleries of Pemberley.

"It is certainly a beautiful feeling to be in love," Lydia said, placing a hand on her stomach. "I had wished for you, my sisters, to find the same kind of love I share with Mr. Wickham."

Neither of the sisters responded as the day before, Lydia had been quite upset that Mr. Wickham had not written to her once since she arrived at Longbourn. But she had soon covered up her disappointment by assuring them all that perhaps he was just too busy bettering their situation before the baby arrived.

It pained Elizabeth that Mr. Wickham did not pay more attention to his wife, especially during the time when she needed him most. Could it be he would have loved and respected her more if she had not so easily agreed to elope with him? Those questions would never be answered because Elizabeth did not plan on further tainting the reputation of the man who was now her brother-in-law. She had to overlook this unpleasant character in order to keep her sister happy and well during her pregnancy. Even though she did not say a word to Lydia's comment, she did pray that perhaps when the baby arrived, Mr. Wickham would find renewed affection for her.

For the sake of the family, and especially Lydia, Elizabeth intended on begging Mr. Darcy to reconcile with Mr. Wickham. But at the moment, she would not bring him up. The mere mention of his name sparked Mr. Darcy's anger, which Elizabeth understood as it was the same kind of anger she harboured towards him.

"Jane," Mary asked, "would you and Mr. Bingley be staying at Netherfield after the wedding?"

"We have not thoroughly discussed the topic of living arrangements, but he did make mention of the fact that we might spend a few months there before purchasing a home not too far from Mr. Darcy and Lizzy."

Kitty sighed. "I would be awfully lonely not to have any of you close by."

"Kitty," Elizabeth placed a hand on that of her younger sister. "You will always be welcome to visit any of us as often as you like. In fact, I shall prepare a room for you to make you feel even more at home."

"Of course you will visit us… all of us." Jane opened her arms wide for Kitty to enter into her embrace. "We shall make every effort to prevent any kind of distance from keeping us apart."

With tears in their eyes, the sisters embraced one another and soon after, they went to bed.

Before falling asleep, Elizabeth kept her eyes open, staring into the darkness, unable to believe that she had found love in a man she had once found to be so proud and unlovable. The changes inside her towards him had completely taken her by surprise. So overwhelmed was she by her love for Mr. Darcy that she had come to slowly heal from the betrayal she had experienced at the hands of the prince who never was. She fell asleep still thinking of Mr. Darcy and their wedding day.

In the morning, she woke up excited to be seeing Mr. Darcy at dinner in the evening, but she soon found it was not only her looking forward to the evening. Everyone in the Bennet household, including the servants who were being ordered around by Mrs. Bennet, were in high spirits until shortly before the guests were expected to arrive.

One of their servants walked into the sitting room, eyes wide with horror as she announced that there was a visitor at the door.

"Mr. Darcy and Mr. Bingley are here already?" Mrs. Bennet asked. "We did not hear the carriage."

"I'm afraid it is another visitor. He would not say his name." She twisted her hands together. "It looks as though he walked."

"Please show the visitor in," Mr. Bennet said, frowning.

"But, Mr. Bennet, we cannot allow

strangers to enter our home."

Mr. Bennet waved a dismissive hand. "It could be someone who has lost their way and needs our assistance."

When the guest arrived in the doorway of the sitting room, silence fell over the room as everyone stared at the man who was barely recognizable with unkempt hair and beard, and filthy, torn clothing.

"The prince–" Mrs. Bennet attempted to rise to her feet but was unable to keep herself upright. She sank back into the chair.

"He is not a prince, Mama," Elizabeth could not help saying, her eyes trained on the face of the man who had once called himself Prince Gabriel, the man who had fooled her into almost making one of the biggest mistakes of her life.

Instead of calling him Andrew, the name she had heard him claim, she decided she would stick to *stranger* instead. After what he had done, that was all he was to her now. Elizabeth was surprised that he had not left town, or had he done so and then returned?

"You lied to me. You lied to all of us,"

Elizabeth said. "I overheard the conversation with your sister at the gallery."

"What are you doing here?" Mr. Bennet asked, standing up to his full height. "I am sure you understand that you are no longer welcome in this house."

"I have come to apologize." The stranger's words were too slurred to be heard clearly. Even from where she sat, Elizabeth was able to detect the smell of strong spirits and the stench of his unwashed body that tainted the air.

The stranger leaned against the doorframe, too intoxicated to stand upright. He did not seem at all surprised that his lies had come to light. Perhaps he had wanted Elizabeth to find out as a way to hurt her after she rejected him.

Mrs. Bennet covered her face with her handkerchief, shaking so much that Jane went to place an arm around her shoulders. She could not bear to look at the man she had once adored and wished for her daughter.

"I would have to ask you to leave," Mr. Bennet said, his voice hard. "Please do not show your face here again."

"I cannot stay away." The stranger turned to look at Elizabeth. "I admit I do not have much, Miss Bennet, but I have plenty of love for you inside my heart. No man will ever love you as much as I do."

"You are wrong, sir," a booming voice sounded from the corridor, moments before Mr. Darcy suddenly appeared behind the stranger, who spun around and almost tripped. "Unlike yours, the love I feel for Elizabeth is untainted with lies. It is honest, and it is real."

As Mr. Darcy spoke, Mr. Bingley's face also came into view. How did they arrive without being heard? The two men now stood on both sides of the stranger.

"Mr. Bennet asked you to leave," Mr. Darcy said as his hands clenched and unclenched at his sides. He was trying hard to keep his temper under control. "It is in your best interest for you to do so."

"If you know what's good for you," the stranger snarled, "you would get out of my way." He curled his hand into a fist and several screams rang out in the room when he swung it at Mr. Darcy. But Mr. Darcy, at seeing what was coming, ducked just in time. As soon as he collected himself, sooner than the stranger, both he and Mr. Bingley apprehended him. They escorted him out of the house with everyone following.

Outside, the stranger attacked not only Mr. Darcy but the whole of the Bennet family with curses and insults of the worst kind. But soon, he threw himself to the ground in tears and looked up at all of them with pleading eyes, telling them he had nowhere to go, and no money to pay for his accommodation at the Rosewood Inn, where he had been staying.

"If you help me pay my bill at the inn, I shall never bother you again." He paused. "You have my word."

Upon hearing his words, Mrs. Bennet suddenly recovered from her sadness and berated him for daring to blackmail them, but Mr. Darcy assured her he would handle it.

"I shall pay all your bills at the inn, but you shall not spend one more night in Hertfordshire. This very night, I will arrange for transportation out of town, but only if you promise to never show your face again."

The stranger started to cry again and crawled up to Mr. Darcy, profusely thanking him. "You are very kind."

"Do not misunderstand me," Mr. Darcy said, stepping away. "I am not doing this out of the goodness of my heart. I am merely protecting my wife-to-be and her family from you."

With that, Mr. Darcy and Mr. Bingley helped the stranger into their carriage and escorted him from the Longbourn house. When they returned a while later, they confirmed that the stranger had left and would never return.

Although they were all still shaken by the visit, they ate dinner together and eventually mustered up the excitement for the weddings, which soon approached.

With renewed respect and love for Mr. Darcy, Elizabeth finally married the man that had been meant for her all along, the man who had arrived in her life with a mask that hid his kindness and love to the world.

Although Lady Catherine did not attend

her nephew's wedding, Anne—her daughter—was present to wish them well, and as luck would have it, among the other guests, she met a suitor of her own.

Jane, as well, had found her happiness in Mr. Bingley, overjoyed that she had not lost him, after all.

After marrying on the same day, the two Bennet sisters created a bond even stronger than the one they had already shared.

As was to be expected, their weddings were the talk of town for a long time, much to Mrs. Bennet's delight.

After the celebrations, both married couples remained at Netherfield until Lydia gave birth to her daughter, Lavinia.

While Elizabeth and Jane had found their happiness, Lydia and Mr. Wickham's situation had worsened. Lydia found herself and the baby spending much of their time at Longbourn, while Mr. Wickham amused himself in Bath or London. He did eventually reappear and profusely apologized to Lydia for the way he had treated her during her pregnancy. He promised her that he was ready to be a better husband and needed her and the baby to return home with him.

The day they rode away from Longbourn, Elizabeth wondered whether he would stay a changed man for good or if he would return to his old ways as soon as life's complications settled upon them.

Soon after the excitement of the new baby had dissipated, everyone continued on with their lives, especially Mrs. Bennet, who turned her attention to Kitty, her only unmarried daughter. She would not rest until the desire to marry off all her girls had been fulfilled.

While she busied herself with finding suitors for Kitty, Mr. Bennet visited Elizabeth at Pemberley as often as he possibly could.

As for Elizabeth and Mr. Darcy, they thanked God for their good fortune and created the kind of marriage many could only dream of.

THE END

Thank you for reading. If you enjoyed this book please consider writing a review, and recommend it to friends and family.

For more information contact:
gracehollisterbooks@gmail.com

Made in the USA
Las Vegas, NV
24 January 2022